Harri Nykänen, born in Helsinki in 1953, was a well-known crime journalist before turning to fiction. He won the Clue Award for Finnish crime writing in 1990 and in 2001. His fiction exposes the local underworld through the eyes of the criminal, the terrorist and, most recently, from the point of view of an eccentric Helsinki police inspector called Ariel Kafka. This is the second in the Ariel Kafka series to appear in English. It follows on from the success of *Nights of Awe*.

Also available from Bitter Lemon Press
by Harri Nykänen:

Nights of Awe

BEHIND GOD'S BACK

Harri Nykänen

Translated by Kristian London

BITTER LEMON PRESS
LONDON

BITTER LEMON PRESS

First published in the United Kingdom in 2015 by
Bitter Lemon Press,
47 Wilmington Square, London WC1X 0ET

www.bitterlemonpress.com

First published in Finnish as *Jumalan selän takana*
by Werner Söderström Corporation (WSOY), Helsinki, 2009

Bitter Lemon Press gratefully acknowledges the
financial assistance of FILI – Finnish Literature
Exchange and the WSOY Literary Foundation

FINNISH LITERATURE EXCHANGE

A CIP record for this book is available
from the British Library

ISBN 978–1–908524–423
eBook ISBN 978–1–908524–430

Typeset by Tetragon, London
Printed and bound by CPI Group (UK) Ltd, Croydon, CR0 4YY

PROLOGUE

After continuing for a month, Operation Jaffa joined that echelon of rare Security Police operations about which exaggerated tales would have been told to grandchildren, had it only been allowed. One could predict the same sort of legendary glow for Jaffa as the battles of the eastern front held for veterans of World War II, or the round-the-clock monitoring of the Soviet embassy (known as *Hustler* duty) held for the old-timers from the Security Police.

Three weeks into the operation, some investigator on a five-cup coffee high invented a new name for it in the quiet hours of the night. And like a bad case of athlete's foot, it immediately spread into common use. On paper the operation continued to be known as Jaffa, but in the field it had a less dignified appellation: Operation Haemorrhoid.

The nickname was like a shortcut across a lawn. Using it was forbidden, but prohibitions and interdictions proved completely ineffective at preventing trespassers. In such cases, it was wisest to give up or build an impassably high fence.

The appropriateness of the name was revealed the first time you spent a few hours without a break on the hard-edged, unpadded kitchen chair.

The two-room flat with a kitchenette had been rented solely for Operation Jaffa. One room was furnished with a folding bed and two stools; the other, which looked out onto the street, contained a table covered in coffee-cup rings, as well as the aforementioned kitchen chair and a couple of its siblings. The chair had been set up in front of the window. A tripod stood next to it, holding a powerful video camera equipped with a spotting scope. The window was covered by a screen of blinds, and a floor-to-ceiling stretch of dark fabric hung behind the chair. Anyone in dark clothes sitting at the window was almost impossible to spot from outside.

A glance through the telescope revealed that it was trained on a storefront across the street. Nothing on the window or door of the storefront indicated what sort of enterprise was contained within its walls. Officially, Cemicon Ltd., a representative of the Israeli chemical industry, operated on the premises. Its product selection included motor oil additives, rust inhibitors and insecticides.

The company had only one employee: the Israeli citizen Leo Meir. Meir did not have a permanent residence, so he lived at his place of business. Which was precisely why the decision had been made to watch the property twenty-four hours a day.

Despite the fact that Meir had an interesting background, the Finnish Security Police wouldn't have gone through the trouble of opening a file on him and setting up a dedicated operation had they not received a tip from the intelligence contact at the US Embassy. According to "reliable sources", Leo Meir was in Helsinki to lay the groundwork for a high-profile assassination.

Unfortunately, though, even the omnipotent CIA did not know whom Meir was supposed to kill. All they knew was that he was under orders to act by mid-September.

That gave the Security Police a little over a month to find the target and stop the murder.

1

I used up my fifteen minutes of fame in the first week of August. Within a three-day period, I was interviewed by morning television, the evening news, a radio talk show and the tabloids. I felt like a VIP, and waited for the notoriety to rush to my head.

I quickly came to find that fame has its advantages. The old sourpuss from downstairs gave me something resembling a smile, and when I rode the tram in to work, a good-looking young woman shot interested glances my way.

I could almost understand those people who sold their self-respect and their souls for a pittance on *Big Brother, Fear Factor*, or one of those other degrading television shows.

I had to admit to myself, though, that my popularity was due to of a string of coincidences. It all began when Seeds of Hate, an extremist organization that had sprung up out of nowhere, kidnapped and assaulted a professor who was researching racism at the University of Helsinki. The bruised and battered scholar had been found wandering the woods north of the city in his underwear.

The case was an unusual one in Finland. The lead investigator was Detective Kari Takamäki from the neighbouring unit, but Takamäki, who coached his son's ice hockey team, took off for Iceland and vanished. Apparently the volcanic soil and magnetic fields prevented cell phones from functioning properly. Either that, or Iceland's teleoperators were as deeply troubled as their banks. Takamäki remained unreachable.

Meanwhile, my supervisor, the head of the Violent Crimes Unit, was in New York on a romantic getaway with his girlfriend.

From a suite in his high-rise Manhattan hotel, he ordered me to handle communications on the case. Chief Detective Huovinen thought I was the right man for the job, since the kidnapped professor was a Jew – just like me.

Apparently Seeds of Hate harboured a particular animosity for us, as half a dozen prominent Jews had received abusive, threatening letters signed by the organization. Still, not even the Security Police knew who the individual or individuals behind Seeds of Hate were. The investigation had got nowhere.

My fame evaporated as quickly as it had materialized. Takamäki emerged from his cell phone dead zone and reassumed responsibility for communications. I took my vacation, which I had split up into three stretches: two in the summer and the third in winter. That gave me something to look forward to.

For some people, the first Monday after a long summer vacation is deathly depressing. For me, it wasn't any more so than any other day. I had already taken two weeks of vacation in May, then these three weeks in August. When I came back to work, it was the end of the month and only a few magical, dew-misted nights from autumn – not that autumn was like the autumns of my childhood any more: the Finnish school year, in defiance of all natural laws, began in August now.

Since despite my family's matchmaking attempts I remained a bachelor, and thus a creature verging on the pathetic, my brother Eli had invited me to his summer cottage – which the world *cottage* was twenty times too modest to describe. I guess he figured I would soak up influences that would spark a desire for the family life. After all, establishing a family and reproducing are central tenets of Jewish existence; they are commandments given by God to man, and not to be shirked. Jewish parents live more for their children, grandchildren and great-grandchildren than for themselves. The future is more important than the present, and without children, there is no future.

I was able to stand Eli for almost a week. I came back to town and lolled around for the next seven days. During my final week of vacation, the weather was gorgeous, so I spent it at sidewalk cafes, reading late, watching rental movies and sleeping in. It was exactly what vacations were originally supposed to be: completely pointless, but relaxing.

The Tuesday that followed the Monday was ordinary, too. I cleared my desk of the mail and preliminary investigative material that had accumulated there during my time off.

On Wednesday, my work began in earnest.

I was just about to head downstairs to eat when my boss stepped into my office. Chief Detective Huovinen was in his shirtsleeves, but he was wearing a sharp-looking bronze-coloured tie. A former male model, Huovinen always looked polished down to the tips of his toes, as an old-fashioned style guide might say.

"You just got a gig. Take Simolin with you and head out to Tammisalo. It should be right up your alley."

"How so?"

"Half an hour ago a man was shot at his front door. Evidently the perpetrator was pretending to be a police officer."

"And what makes it up my alley?"

Huovinen folded his arms across his chest and frowned. "The victim's name is Samuel Jacobson. You know him?"

"Yes."

Jacobson owned a chain of office supply stores. He was also prominently involved in the activities of Helsinki's Jewish community. He was over twenty years older than me, so I mostly knew him through the congregation. He had played soccer at the national level as a young man. When I was eighteen, I had dated his daughter Lea for a few months; she and I went to the same high school. It didn't take long for me to realize that Samuel Jacobson had absolutely no desire to become my father-in-law. I haven't had much luck on the son-in-law market since.

"It can't hurt the investigation that you know Jacobson and his circle – at least better than anybody else on the force. Jacobson must have got mixed up in something. He wasn't robbed, and the perpetrator clearly wasn't some crazy junkie killer who just happened to end up on his doorstep. Seems like a tricky case. Does Jacobson have a family?"

"A wife and two kids, a son and a daughter. The son works in the family business, the daughter lives abroad."

I considered whether or not I should mention that I had dated Lea, and decided not to.

"OK. Take the case, then… unless there's some reason why you can't… something I should know about."

"Nope."

On the way to eastern Helsinki, I spent a minute reflecting on Huovinen's question. Helsinki's Jewish community was small, and all of its members more or less knew each other. That was no reason to excuse myself from the case. All the residents of a small town know each other, too, and that doesn't disqualify the local police from doing their jobs. Still, a boss other than Huovinen might have suspected Jews of having some secret pact of mutual assistance, something that would prevent them from telling the truth if another Jew were involved in a case.

My relationship with Lea had come to an abrupt end when someone blabbed that, after a party at my friend's, I had stayed behind with Karmela Mayer, the daughter of the fur shop owner. I had dated Karmela for over a year, and had almost ended up under the *chuppah*. Karmela lived in Israel these days, and had three children. I still had restless dreams about her large breasts. Lea also moved to Israel later and married a wealthy entrepreneur, or at least that's what I remembered someone telling me. That's the extent of what I knew about her family life.

I had dated three other Jewish girls and screwed up those relationships, too. When you added one-night stands, if you wanted to draw a hard line, I was disqualified when it came to every single Jewish family in Helsinki.

Detective Simolin drove in silence, looking a little uncomfortable. He probably blamed himself for my reticence. Simolin was a good police officer, but so inherently innocent that he often found himself coming up against life's realities. He was fascinated by North American Indians. He even had an Indian name, which he wouldn't tell anyone, and a set of buckskins complete with moccasins and a feathered headdress. He also had a genuine Indian bow and a steady hand. Simolin would have never confused the Crees of the northern plains with the Crows of the central plains because he was an expert on Indian tribes, their territories and ways of life. In addition, he was an enthusiastic astronomer, and had built his own reflecting telescope. Had he lived in the '50s, it was easy to imagine him devouring those hobby magazines for boys and building all the gadgets they featured: rudimentary receivers, soapbox radios and microscopes. But these days, such enthusiasm was old-fashioned and naive.

"Huovinen told me that Jacobson was Jewish. Do you know him?" Simolin asked.

"Yeah. Not well, but a little. I used to date his daughter back in the day, but only for a few months."

"Really?" Simolin sounded excited. "I've heard his name somewhere. Was he retired?"

"Not that I know of."

Simolin frowned. "Huh. Then what was he doing at home in the middle of the day?"

"Beats me."

The thought hadn't even crossed my mind. But it had crossed Simolin's, and before continuing he paused for a moment, as if waiting to hear my opinion of his observation before offering his own. Simolin wasn't ambitious that way. He let others shine.

"It occurred to me that the murderer might have been dressed like a policeman because Jacobson was afraid of something and wouldn't have opened the door otherwise. And that's why he didn't go to work either."

"Jacobson didn't strike me as the type that anyone would want to kill."

"And yet someone did," Simolin pointed out. "And in a police uniform, too. I had time to do a little checking – there are three known cases in Finland where a police officer's uniform has gone missing. That's not very many. Two were in the Helsinki area, one in Lapland."

"If it even was a police uniform. People think anyone in a dark-blue uniform and a cap is a police officer."

"True enough," Simolin admitted.

"You already take your vacation?" I asked, after we drove a moment longer in silence. We were just passing through the neighbourhood of Herttoniemi.

"Two weeks. I'm saving the rest for winter. I'm going to travel to the States for two weeks."

"Alone?"

Simolin appeared to be blushing.

"With my girlfriend… We're going to go visit this one Indian tribe. They have a big celebration around that time. Everyone dresses in traditional ceremonial garb, and the men perform the buffalo dance. It's not your run-of-the-mill tourist show."

"That must be an amazing experience."

"I've been saving up for this trip for almost two years."

I knew that Simolin didn't discuss his Indian pursuits with anyone at work except me. Maybe he figured that, being a Jew, I understood other minorities. But the fact was I had never poked fun at his interest in Indians. Sometimes we'd talk about the stars and space, too.

The infinity of the universe impressed everyone, but it aroused endless awe and admiration in Simolin. Words never sufficed to explain what he'd seen the previous night through his reflector telescope. He'd spotted the rings of Saturn, or the Horsehead Nebula of Orion. Such things reminded you how small and finite man's existence truly is, Simolin had confessed during one late-night shift.

"Did Jacobson have a family?" he asked. "Oh, that's right, you dated his daughter."

"Wife and two grown children."

"Do you want me to talk to the daughter if there's still something between you guys? Or maybe Arja can? She's coming out, too."

"Lea's still in Israel. Besides, it's not a very delicate subject any more. It's been over twenty years."

We turned towards Tammisalo, leaving Herttoniemi Manor behind to the right. The Jacobsons had lived in Tammisalo back when I dated Lea, and on several occasions we had taken walks in the manor grounds. It had been August, and there on the lawn, under cover of the balmy darkness, I tried to get into her pants. Even though things always started out promisingly, Lea would eventually put on the brakes. My efforts weren't rewarded until a little before our relationship came to an end. It had been at the Jacobson summer cottage in Emäsalo, where we spent a weekend without old man Jacobson's knowledge.

As I took in the familiar scenery, I remembered how I used to ride the blue Tammisalo Transit bus to pick up Lea. Back then, it had felt like I was travelling to the countryside: the houses had been old and dilapidated and their orchards large. Now they had been subdivided, and the road was lined with brick homes, each one grander than the next.

We crossed the bridge, circled the roundabout, and turned towards the shore.

"Pull up next to that fence," I told Simolin. The Jacobson residence was a boxy, flat-roofed brick house built in the 1970s. Samuel Jacobson had commissioned it himself, and in the end he died in the doorway of his own home. Much to my surprise, he was still lying there.

Two patrol cars and a tech van stood in the drive. I could see an elderly couple peering out of the windows of the house next door. You couldn't miss the woman's silvery hair. Evidently they were the eyewitnesses to the crime.

I didn't want to disturb the CSIs right when they were busiest. The sky was growing dark and threatening rain. A downpour wouldn't do anything to further the technical investigation.

The deceased was lying on his left side, head towards the front door. He was dressed in dark-blue cotton trousers and a lightweight sweater. The door was wide open, and I could see an investigator going about her business in the hallway. Someone else was taking a photograph inside.

I touched Simolin's sleeve. "Let's go have a chat with the neighbours."

They were expecting us; the door opened before I could ring the bell. The man and grey-haired woman who had just been standing at the window were peering out through the crack. I introduced Simolin and myself, and the man asked us in.

A mid-length fur coat was hanging in the hallway, then the family dog trotted in and started sniffing at my feet. It was small and white and fluffy; I didn't recognize the breed. My nose started to itch and I could feel a sneeze coming on. I was allergic to animal fur, which was one reason the relationship between me and Mr Mayer's daughter had withered on the vine. Both Old Man Mayer and Karmela had wanted me to take over the fur shop.

I got right to the point. "Which one of you saw the assailant?"

"Kalevi, my husband, did," said the woman.

"So you didn't see him at all?"

"I saw him sitting in the car, but by that time it was too late to tell if he was a policeman or not."

"What about the vehicle? What can you tell us about that?" Simolin asked. The man leant in. Now we had entered his area of expertise.

"It was a dark-blue Volkswagen Golf, no doubt about it. Isn't that what the police drive? There weren't any police markings on it, but there was a blue light on the roof… Or wait, I wouldn't bet my life on that; it was behind the bushes and I could only see part of it. But there was definitely something on the roof. I didn't see the licence plate."

"Could you tell us what else you saw? Start from the beginning, and tell us everything."

"I didn't see the incident itself – the murder, I mean. I went to the window to have a look once Titi started barking. Titi has her very own chair set up there, because she's a curious little girl. So I heard her barking and went to have a look. Through my binoculars, I could see Jacobson lying in the doorway and a man who looked like a police officer walking away. Kaarina was upstairs and I yelled for her to come down. The second she got here, the man drove off. Ooh, I was miffed at her, but Kaarina's legs aren't too good."

"Yours are even worse," his wife huffed.

"Which is why I was downstairs."

The man showed us the binoculars that were on the hallway table.

"I had these. I looked out the window to see what had happened to my neighbour, and I could see there was blood on his face. I phoned an ambulance right then and there, and they called the police when I told them what had happened."

"So the man was dressed like a police officer?"

"That's what it looked like. Blue uniform and a cap. He had badges on his chest and his sleeve that looked like police badges to me, you know, the sword and everything."

"So you didn't see the actual shooting?"

"No, but who else could it have been? No one would leave someone lying in a pool of blood unless they were the guilty party."

"No doubt you're right about that. What about the shot?"

"I definitely would have heard a shot. There's nothing wrong with my hearing. The murderer must have been a professional. They use silencers." Now Kalevi was getting excited.

"So you didn't see the gun?" Simolin asked.

"No. That darned bush was right in the way."

"Was Jacobson often home in the middle of the day?"

The woman shook her head. "No, he wasn't."

Her husband agreed: "Not a chance. Jacobson was a workaholic. Owned a chain of office supply shops. Inherited it from his father and expanded it quite a bit. Must have at least twenty employees. Jews have a nose for business."

"What about recently? Was he home yesterday? Or the day before?"

"I think he was. Yes, he was. Now that I think about it, he's been home for at least three to four days. Which is a little odd, because he didn't seem ill. Usually if he's ill, his wife stays home to tend to him. The kids have already flown the coop, of course."

"How well do you know the Jacobsons?" I asked.

"As well as neighbours do after having lived next door to each other for close to thirty years. We used to visit each other now and again, but because we're of different generations that was the extent of it. The Jacobsons have been good neighbours: never make a fuss and keep the yard tidy. The children were always polite, too."

"Did Jacobson ever mention receiving any threats?"

"No," the man sighed. "He got along with everyone, at least here in Tammisalo. Belonged to the neighbourhood association, may have even been on the board. Who would want to threaten him?"

"Someone killed him," Simolin pointed out.

"Yes, that's true," the man said thoughtfully. "You don't kill someone for no reason, so the murderer must have had one."

"Do you have any idea what it might have been?"

"No, unless it has to do with him being a Jew – maybe one of those Nazis or terrorists or what have you that hates their kind…" The man glanced at me and must have put together my name, my appearance and my ethnic background. "It's just that it's been happening lately. They beat up that foreign professor, too. Can't think of anything else."

"And you never saw anyone suspicious snooping around the house?"

"Nothing but apple thieves. This time of year the kids go around raiding orchards – not as much as they used to, though. You almost wish they would, with the apples rotting on the ground and all…"

"What kind of people live around here?"

"Good people. Over on the other side of the Jacobsons', there's a hockey player who spends most of the year abroad, in the US. Their house has been empty for over a month. No one lives up across the street. An older couple used to live there. He died five years ago, and then she passed two years later. The heirs plan to sell the land, and I guess the house will be torn down, because it's in pretty bad shape. Back in the day, it was the pride of the neighbourhood: huge rosebushes and flowerbeds, cherries, apples, plums and pears. The man had quite the green thumb. Now the yard is so overgrown you can't even see the house from here any more."

I had noticed the home on the hill when we drove up. Its former beauty was still evident, as was that of the yard, even though the grounds were overgrown and the house was falling apart. There was no doubt that the plot, over twenty-thousand square feet, was worth a bundle.

"Do all the neighbours know each other?"

"Everyone except the hockey player are old Tammisalo locals, have lived here as long as we have… It's a shame. Jacobson and I exchanged a couple of words a few weeks back, and he said he intended to retire at the end of the year and leave the company to his children. Sad. Didn't have a chance to enjoy a single day of his retirement. One thing's for sure: death comes like a thief in the night. You never know whether you have an hour left, or ten years."

I left my card with the man, who was lost in philosophical reverie, and asked them to get in touch if something came up.

As we walked back over to the Jacobson property, a TV news van pulled up in front of the house. The cameraman and a crime reporter I knew climbed out and walked in our direction.

"Can we shoot the yard?"

"At your own risk. Privacy laws apply to the entire property, as you well know."

The reporter looked disappointed. Then she told the cameraman to get a few panoramas of the road, the house and the police car.

"We know that the resident was shot at his front door. What else can you tell us?"

"I don't know any more than you do."

The reporter looked sceptical. "Do you have anything on the motive? Was it a robbery, for instance?"

"Doesn't appear to be, but we're looking into it. We'll send out a press release this afternoon once we get something together."

A silver Audi was approaching the house. I had seen Jacobson drive it before and knew that it was his wife, Ethel. Facing the loved ones of the deceased was never easy, and it was even less so if you happened to know them and like them. During that brief period when I had spent some time at the Jacobson household, I had liked Lea's mother more than her father. Ethel was a couple of years younger than her husband. Her family was originally from Gdansk, Poland, but had lived in Turku since the '50s. We hadn't seen each other in years, because neither Ethel nor I were very zealous synagogue attendees, and since no familial bond existed, where else would we have run into each other?

I threw a warning glance at the reporter, even though I didn't think that either she or the cameraman would ambush Ethel. "Keep your distance, and think before you shoot."

I crossed into the yard to wait. Ethel scratched the side of her car against the gatepost, but didn't even seem to notice. She jumped out and lunged for the stairs, where her husband lay waiting under a white sheet. It was like footage from those news clips of war-zone tragedies I'd seen a hundred times. Ethel clutched her husband and held him in her arms as she knelt there on the landing, wailing and rocking the body, face turned heavenwards. Her blazer and shirt were stained with blood, and she was looking off somewhere in the distance beyond me. The emptiness of her gaze frightened me. I touched her shoulder, but she didn't react in the least.

"Ethel. Do you remember me? It's Ariel. Ariel Kafka. I used to date Lea."

Ethel startled me by grabbing my hand and squeezing it so hard it hurt.

"Ariel. You naughty man… Why haven't you been to see me or Lea?"

I helped her up and she immediately collapsed into my arms, weeping and rambling. "Why did they kill Samuel? He was a good man. You liked him, too, didn't you, Ariel…?"

"Of course I did."

I led Ethel inside, because there was no point trying to ask her anything while she was standing next to her husband's body. Sensitive Simolin followed at a discreet distance. He was a singularly inconspicuous civil servant.

Once inside, Ethel was able to detach herself from what had happened, and began thinking about practical matters. "I have to call Roni. Roni's in Lapland… and Lea's in Israel… Both the children are away when their father dies…"

She was cut off by a gush of tears, but it didn't take her long to pull herself together.

"I'd like to ask a few questions. It's important that we get the investigation started as quickly as possible. Do you think you can you manage that?"

"Of course. Luckily, you're a good detective and you'll find whoever did this. Ask whatever you need to." Ethel blew into her handkerchief, and looked at me expectantly.

"Your husband stayed home from work for several days. Why was that, even though apparently he wasn't ill?"

"I don't know."

"But his absence from work was not due to illness, is that correct?"

"That's correct."

"And you don't know the cause?"

"Of course I asked him. He said he had his reasons, but that he couldn't talk to me about them. I was worried, because work is so important to him… I tried my best to get him to explain what was going on, but he wouldn't budge. He could be a stubborn man. He wouldn't let me help, his own wife…"

I continued questioning before her emotions got the best of her again.

"How many days had he been away from work?"

"Three."

I glanced around. The living room looked almost exactly the same as it had twenty years earlier, with the exception of a new flat-screen television in place of the old TV and a couple of striking bronze sculptures standing on the floor. But the sofa was the same one where I had tried to warm up Lea on the few evenings we had spent out from under the watchful gaze of her parents.

"And you don't have the slightest idea what it could have been about?"

"No. I thought so hard I couldn't sleep and my imagination started conjuring up all kinds of strange ideas, but in the morning I understood they were complete nonsense."

"I'd still like to hear them."

"At first I thought Samuel had written something that had angered those crazy racists. I kept telling him to think twice before he wrote but —"

"Where did he write?"

"For *Hakehila*."

Hakehila was the publication of the Helsinki Jewish congregation.

"Then I thought he had embezzled money and was too ashamed to go in to work... Until I realized that you can't embezzle from yourself, can you?" Ethel laughed bitterly. "It even crossed my mind that he may have had some ugly affair at the office, and that the woman's husband was threatening him."

"Affair? Was he involved with one of his employees?"

"No, but I imagined he was. He had several attractive women working for him."

"Did he seem anxious?"

"I asked him if had done something that was forcing him to hide. He denied it. I still thought he was afraid, though. He tried to act as if everything was normal, but I noticed that he'd walk over to the window from time to time and look out, and he tested the door several times a day to make sure it was locked. He told me not to let in anyone I didn't know. It wasn't until I asked him why that he told me he might be in danger. He wouldn't say any more than that."

"Did anything else come to mind besides racists or a husband who had been cheated on?"

"My mind was on a roller coaster. I thought it was one thing, then something else. In the end I decided it was money... Maybe he'd had a disagreement with someone over money, a deal or something like that... Maybe someone felt like they had been cheated."

"How did he respond?"

"He said it wasn't about money. For him, life was too short to argue about money."

I had a slightly different view of Jacobson's philosophy of life, but this wasn't the right time to discuss it.

I took Ethel's hand and gave it a consoling squeeze. It was well manicured; the back of her palm was soft as chamois. It was the hand of an ageing woman.

"I'm sorry, but I need to ask you some unpleasant questions. Is it possible that Samuel had any gambling debts?"

"Not in a million years," Ethel huffed. "Samuel wouldn't even play bridge, no matter how hard I tried to get him to. Gambling didn't interest him in the least."

"Might he have been mixed up in something criminal, financed a project that later turned out to be criminal?"

"Neither he nor the company had enough money to fund criminal activity. Ariel, I'll be honest with you... Building our own office building was Samuel's biggest mistake. We did it right at the peak of the construction market, and it cost five million euros, two of which were borrowed. The building was finished three years ago, but anything extra still goes to paying off the construction loans. Meanwhile, turnover has dropped and things are getting worse and worse. Samuel was worried about that, because he had promised Roni that he would turn over directorship to him at the end of the year. The whole reason Samuel wanted the new building was that it was important to him that Roni have a successful business to run, like the one he had received from his father. Roni and Lea were everything to him. Which is why he decided to stay on as CEO until it was back on its feet..."

Ethel's self-control began to crumble, but I had to press on. The previous question had laid the foundation for the one I wanted to ask next. "What if he had been forced to fund criminal activity for the very reason that he wouldn't have been able to manage the loans otherwise?"

"Oh, things weren't that tight for us. And he meant to take out a new loan from a Finnish bank and pay off the old one. He said he'd had a better loan offer."

"When?"

"A couple of weeks ago."

"Where did the old loan come from?"

"I don't know."

"You don't? But you worked for the company, too, didn't you, in accounting?"

Tears were streaming down Ethel's cheeks, and she didn't even try to wipe them away.

"Do you know what the worst thing is, Ariel? We parted in strife. I gave him a piece of my mind this morning… But how could I have known, you never know… which is why you should always part as friends. When we started dating, we agreed that we would never go to bed until we had settled any arguments…"

I gave her a minute to calm down and repeated: "You also worked for the company. Shouldn't you have known about the loan, too?"

"All I know is that the loan was brokered by Samuel's friend and the money came from Estonia, but from which bank, I couldn't tell you. The broker held on to the paperwork."

"Why didn't he take out a loan from a Finnish bank?"

"He said you could get a loan from Estonia at a lower interest rate. I didn't argue, because I knew the broker. You know him pretty well yourself."

"Who are you talking about?"

"Oxbaum. He represents the Estonian bank here in Finland."

"Max Oxbaum?"

"Yes."

Max Oxbaum was a well-known attorney, my second cousin and my brother Eli's business partner. Together they owned a law firm named Kafka & Oxbaum.

2

By now at the latest I could have excused myself from the case, and with good cause. But I didn't want to. No matter what was revealed during the investigation, my brother would answer for his deeds. If a collision with my brother's actions looked inevitable, I would step aside at the last minute and, if necessary, hand anything involving him over to another investigator.

Eli was a successful corporate lawyer and had married into money, too. There had been a time when I had been almost envious of my brother, who, along with a good wife, had two sharp kids, a swanky apartment in Eira, a German luxury vehicle, a summer villa the size of a manor and a position of respect in the Jewish congregation. I had none of the above. On the other hand, my brother was four years older and three inches shorter than me, and ran to fat. Plus there was a bald spot on his head where his hair had just begun to thin.

I knew from before that Eli and Max's law office brokered their clients' loans from an Estonian company, Baltic Invest. Baltic Invest was owned by an Israeli businessman named Benjamin Hararin. I had heard all of this from my childhood friend Dan just before his death. According to Dan, who had worked for the Mossad, Hararin's affairs were being investigated in Israel because he was suspected of laundering money for the Russian mafia. Dan had also hinted that Hararin was in possession of sensitive video material starring Eli and Max.

I had reported my intelligence to the financial crimes division of the National Bureau of Investigation. The NBI had requested further information from the Israeli police, but received no response – not even confirmation of the investigation's existence.

I had looked into the matter myself using my own sources and the Internet. I discovered that Hararin, himself a millionaire, was considered a frontman for a businessman named Amos Jakov. Jakov was among those 140,000 Jews who had emigrated to Israel from the Soviet Union in the '70s. Upon his arrival in 1973, at the age of twenty-two, Jakov initially enlisted in the Israeli army and then the Mossad, where he gained a tough reputation and rose to the middle ranks. Through contacts he apparently acquired during his stint with the Mossad and money that came from Russia, he got into real estate and then expanded into energy. He had particularly good connections in Turkmenistan and Kazakhstan, both of which were rich in oil, gas and minerals. He was considered a good friend of the president of Kazakhstan, and when he acquired a Kazakh chromium mine in the 1990s, it was rumoured that the deal coincided with the transfer of 100 million dollars into the president's Swiss bank accounts. Plenty had been written about Jakov in the international financial press.

In contrast, information on Jakov's mafia contacts was scarce, but some anonymous sources indicated that he had belonged to a local criminal gang in his birth city of Minsk and had been sentenced to prison for assault and robbery. When the Soviet Union collapsed and Minsk became the capital of Belarus, Jakov was able to exploit his old contacts, some of whom later moved to Israel, others to the United States. I found a *New York Times* article that linked FBI investigations of money laundering to Jakov.

Time passed and nothing happened; I had already forgotten about both Eli and Max's business dealings as well as Jakov and Hararin. Now I was faced with the whole mess again. It felt like I had been slapped in the face with a wet rag, and for good reason.

When I stepped out of the Jacobsons' house, Simolin was talking with one of the CSIs in the yard. I joined them.

"Three shells were recovered, and so were two bullets, one in pretty good shape. Dug out of a porch pillar; .22 calibre," Simolin reported.

"What else?" I asked the investigator.

"The shooter must have stayed on the paving, because there aren't any footprints. The shots were fired from within three feet, so there aren't even any traces of contact. We've combed over the entire property but haven't found a thing. There are no tyre marks, either. So basically what we have is a whole lot of nothing. The bullets and shells will tell us the manufacturer and make of the weapon, assuming we find it."

Simolin was doubtful. "Not likely."

"We'll have to talk to the people living along the vehicle's escape route. Someone might have seen something. I'll call in some more support," I said.

"This is when we could use that famous dog-walker who saw the whole thing," Simolin jibed, without the slightest trace of humour.

I stepped aside to phone in the request for more patrols. In the middle of the call, I saw my subordinate Arja Stenman arrive. She looked as classy as ever. To be honest, she looked too classy for rough-and-tumble police work. She would have fit right in as the trophy wife of a middle-ranking CEO. In a way, she had been pretty close. She was divorced, but her ex-husband owned, or had owned, a construction equipment rental company. He had sold it in the nick of time before the police and the tax authorities caught up with him. Stolen machinery had been found in the company's warehouses. In any case, Arja Stenman had been accustomed to a life where you didn't have to worry about whether the money would stretch till payday. She had clear skin, freckles and a straight nose. I couldn't deny it: she was easy on the eyes.

"I called about the car on my way over. Nothing similar has been reported stolen, but it's unlikely that the killer is driving his own vehicle," Stenman said.

"Would you come inside with me?" I said. "Simolin, once more people show up, take the lead in canvassing the neighbours."

The body was just now being transported to the ambulance. As a Jew, Jacobson would receive accelerated handling, because Jews expected to bury their dead within twenty-four hours. If the loved ones lived a long way away, the burial could be postponed for a couple of days. Every Jewish congregation had its own holy society, called a *chevra kadisha*, which took care of burial arrangements.

Of course the burial would be postponed if a criminal investigation demanded storage of the body, but I knew from experience that the *chevra kadisha* knew how to pull the right strings to inter the body within their preferred time frame. Autopsies weren't even conducted unless specifically demanded by the investigation. Jacobson was a pillar of the congregation, and getting him into the ground in the prescribed time would be a matter of honour.

Ethel was sitting on the sofa, talking on the phone. It only took a few words for me to gather she was speaking with her daughter in Israel. She intermittently wiped her eyes as she spoke.

Ari's here... Ariel Kafka... He's investigating your father's... I have to go. Tell Rachel and Dan that Grandma sends them her love... Of course I will."

Ethel rose. "Lea said to say hello. She'll be arriving on the evening flight tomorrow."

"Could I have a look around your husband's office?" I asked.

"Why on earth?"

"Maybe he jotted something down... something that will help us. On his calendar or planner or whatnot. We'll go over to the company later, as well."

"I suppose you know what needs to be done."

Ethel led Stenman and me into the office, although I knew the way. I had a distinct memory of the time Samuel Jacobson asked me to step back there with him, shut the door and lectured me on what was expected of a man who dated his daughter. The list had been a long one: ambition, initiative, responsibility, courage, fidelity, loyalty, respect for traditions, respect for parents...

All of this despite the fact that Lea and I had only been out a few times, and all of my ambition and initiative went into breaking down her moral resistance.

The office was small, and the walls were lined with books, paintings, mementoes and photographs. In one shot, a young-ish Jacobson was shaking hands with Ariel Sharon; in another, with General Moshe Dayan. The photos had been taken during a trip Makkabi made to Israel in the 1970s; Makkabi was the Helsinki Jewish congregation's sports club. There was also a photo of Israeli Prime Minister Golda Meir at the Helsinki Synagogue during her visit to Finland in 1971, and one of defence minister Yitzhak Rabin at the same synagogue in 1986.

In one of the snapshots, Jacobson was sitting on a rattan couch next to a young man I couldn't identify, despite the fact that he looked familiar. I could identify the setting, though. The photo was taken in the Jacobsons' back yard.

I pointed at the man. "Who's he?" I asked Ethel.

"Haim Levi. He was an exchange student in Finland twenty years ago and lived with us for six months. He was appointed Minister of Justice in Israel not long ago. A very nice young man. He loved Finland, especially our cottage in Emäsalo... Has it really been that long?"

Stenman also came over to have a look. "I've heard of Levi. He's a controversial man in Israel."

"Haim and Roni became very close friends."

I examined the picture. Although in general my feeling was that photos of a host posing with famous guests didn't reveal much aside from the host's self-infatuation, in Samuel's case they also said something about his status in the Helsinki Jewish congregation. He was respected among his own.

There were two more photos on the desk, and Jacobson didn't appear in either of them. One was taken in the back yard some summer long ago. In it, Lea and Roni were in an inflatable yellow pool; they were four or five years old. Roni was a year younger than Lea. In the other shot, they were sitting in a garden swing under some apple trees. This time, they were close to adolescence.

Ethel noticed my gaze and picked up the garden shot. "How time flies... What year was it when you two dated?"

"I was eighteen then, so it was..."

"It was such a lovely time when the children were little," Ethel said, referring to the time before me. "Lea and Roni were never any trouble, bundles of pure joy. Israel is the Holy Land and our God-given homeland, but I still wish Lea hadn't moved so far away. We don't see each other often enough."

Ethel touched my sleeve. I was some link to past bliss, and she didn't want to come back yet. The same kind of link as a crackly old film strip where children run eternally into their father's or mother's arms, take their first steps, learn to ride a bike, ski, swim, where the sun shines through the leaves of the apple trees...

"Lea has two wonderful children, Dan and Rachel. They love visiting their Grandma..."

Stenman's phone rang, breaking the spell. She went into the other room to talk. Ethel looked at me mournfully.

"Samuel was very fond of you..."

I had a completely contrary view of this matter as well. My impression had been that I hadn't met Jacobson's criteria for a son-in-law. I had no trouble remembering his exact expression when he eyed me in this very room twenty-four years earlier. It said that he doubted I was good enough for his daughter. He frowned like a diamond merchant who was being sold a chunk of glass. I probably wouldn't have got along with him very well if he had become my father-in-law. Ethel, on the other hand, I had liked from the start.

"If there's anything here, this is where it would be," Ethel said, opening the desk drawer. "Samuel has a safe at the office. That's where he kept the loan papers and other important company documents."

I rifled through the drawer and found three planners and a notebook. Jacobson was the old-fashioned type. He probably wrote everything important down on paper and left the laptop, which sat closed on the desk, unused. On the other hand, it had to be more than a prop.

The notebook contained mostly names and addresses. I put it down and concentrated on the planner. Jacobson had an average of three meetings a day. The previous week he'd had three lunchtime meetings and a slew of others.

Stenman walked over and pulled me aside. "That was Simolin. A racist threat was found at Jacobson's company. It was in the mail box this morning, but they didn't report it until now, after they heard what had happened."

"Let's head over," I said, and then turned to Ethel. "We'll take these with us, and the laptop, too, if you don't mind. Do you know what your husband used the computer for?"

"He didn't use it much. He'd use the Internet a little, but he wasn't interested in these new fads, even though we sold computers, too. When he started out, we were the largest type-writer retailer in Helsinki. He knew them so well that he would even help out with repairs if there was a rush. That was one of the reasons he wanted to turn over responsibility to Roni."

Ethel went and got two shopping bags for us, and we piled them full of anything of interest from the office.

I was already stepping out of the front door when Ethel said: "Lea will be here tomorrow... I told her you were the investigator... She said she'd like to see you."

"Of course. I'll also have to talk to Roni."

"Why?"

"Maybe your husband told him something."

"He didn't. The first day his dad stayed home from work, Roni called from Lapland and tried to pry, but Samuel was as bull-headed with him as he was with me, wouldn't say a word."

"We still have to speak to all members of the family. You said there was a safe at your husband's office. Who has the keys?"

"I do… and Samuel. I think they're in his coat pocket."

"Could you check, please?"

We followed Ethel back into the hallway. She searched a coat hanging from the rack and found a gleaming set of keys.

"Here they are."

"I'd like to borrow them for a while."

Ethel looked as if she wanted to know what right I had to ask for the keys. Maybe she momentarily forgot that I was a police officer, not some kid who was after her daughter. I held out my hand and, after a moment's hesitation, she dropped the keys into it.

"There's also some money in the safe. Not much, but a small emergency fund."

"Do you mind if I take a look at that coat, please?" Stenman asked.

Ethel reluctantly handed over the coat. Stenman went through the pockets and the wallet she found in the breast pocket: a few business cards and a little over a hundred euros in cash.

"Samuel didn't even have an ATM card. He was afraid some-one would steal it and empty the account," Ethel said.

As we left, I saw Ethel watching us from the window.

"Next stop: Jacobson's office," I said to Stenman.

"You know how to get there?"

"I think I can manage it."

I chose a route that passed by the manor and continued towards Herttoniemi. As we were crossing the bridge between Tammisalo and Herttoniemi, an idea occurred to me.

"Jacobson's killer had to escape either this way or take Tammisalontie to Roihuvuori. Either way, he had to cross a bridge. If I were the killer, I'd toss the weapon into the sea."

"Me too. Should we call in the divers?"

"Definitely."

3

The Jacobson family business had been founded by Samuel Jacobson's father, Ruben Jacobson, back in the 1930s. It imported office machines and supplies. The company had grown rapidly after the war, ballooning from a small office-machine repair shop into a big-time importer. The era was so favourable for expansion that everyone who showed a little initiative did all right for themselves. Ruben Jacobson showed a lot of initiative and did better than all right. He spoke German and English, and managed to secure exclusive import and maintenance rights for a couple of international brands, and that was enough.

When computers burst onto the market in the 1980s, manual and electric typewriters turned into fishing-net weights and scrap metal overnight. That moment almost proved fatal for the company. Ruben didn't think much of computers, and because at the age of seventy-five he was still the chair of the board, his opinion mattered. But Ruben wasn't stupid; it didn't take him long to realize that he had bet on the wrong horse, and he changed course. He stepped aside and turned control over to his only son, Samuel. His daughter lived in Denmark; she wasn't interested in office machines.

The maintenance and repair company that had its start in an old wooden building in a Punavuori courtyard moved to new, more central premises in 1948. In the '50s, Ruben Jacobson bought a bigger space in Vallila, and the firm operated there until Samuel Jacobson commissioned a new building for it in a northern Helsinki industrial area in 2005.

The new building had two stories and a glass-and-aluminium facade. The lower floor contained the storeroom, the repair shop and social areas; the upper floor the offices and conference room.

I learnt the company's history from the brochure I read at the break room table. I knew the rest from before.

Stenman and I were waiting for the company's chief financial officer, who was at some negotiations away from the offices. He had promised to return as soon as possible. It had already been almost twenty minutes.

"If you'd married Jacobson's daughter, you'd be investigating your father-in-law's murder right now," Stenman observed. She had crossed her long, denim-sheathed legs. Her coat was unbuttoned, and underneath there was a pale-blue blouse whose two top buttons were also open. My eyes took in the scenery in spite of the prohibition I had set for myself. "So why didn't you, anyway?" Stenman asked.

"Because I got caught with another woman. It's not as dramatic or sexy as it sounds, but it was enough for Lea. She said she just couldn't respect me any more. We were both eighteen."

"Sounds pretty melodramatic."

"You are when you're eighteen."

"Did you regret it?"

"Not then, and not now. It wasn't even a serious relationship. We were just more feeling things out – with both hands. I knew Lea was looking for a different kind of man."

"Feeling things out with both hands, huh?" Stenman chuckled. "You must have been pretty wild."

"No more so than most kids that age."

"Did she find what she was looking for? She's married and has kids, right?"

"Hopefully. She married a businessman."

"Do you mean that at least she has money?"

"I think that weighed in the balance."

Stenman had divorced a couple of years ago, and had definitely not been left high and dry. She had taken the two children and moved into a large apartment in Kruununhaka. I had been by a couple of times to pick her up for work. You didn't buy a place like that on a detective's salary.

A man approaching sixty walked in. My hunch was that the chief financial officer, Pekka Hulkko, had just arrived. He wiped the sweat from his brow. He must have come in a rush. I stood up.

"I'm sorry you had to wait… It's just that you never imagine that… The letter is in my office."

We followed Hulkko into a room with a view of the tallest building in Vantaa. The letter was in a plastic file organizer.

"No one has touched it since I read it, so we wouldn't leave any fingerprints."

Television police shows were of some use after all.

The contents were brief and to the point, like vitriolic outbursts usually are: "*Greedy fucking Jewish scum. One day you're going to get what you deserve. The Seeds of Hate.*"

No other signatures, or anything else for that matter.

"When did this arrive?"

"It was in the company's mail box this morning. There was nothing on the envelope, so someone came last night or early this morning and left it there."

"Have you ever received anything like this before?"

"Not that I know of. I think Samuel would have told me if we had. He always took matters like this seriously."

A round table stood in the corner, surrounded by four chairs. Hulkko invited us to sit.

"Jacobson didn't come in to work for three days. Do you know why?"

"He called and said he wasn't feeling well. The flu, I guess. It's going around."

"Doesn't it seem odd to you that the threat was delivered here?" Stenman asked.

"How so? Jacobson is a Jew. For some people at least, this is a Jewish company. People who oppose Israel won't even eat Jaffa-brand oranges."

"But Jacobson wasn't especially well known. How did the person who made the threat know he was a Jew in the first place?"

"Those guys know. They read the congregation newsletters and spend time online. And you can guess from the name – the first name, at least."

"We haven't heard about any other similar threats. You'd think they'd have started from the top, from the head of the congregation or the rabbi or some public persona."

"Aren't the police investigating that Seeds of Hate group? You'd think that'd be the place they'd start looking for the perpetrator."

"The other letters are different. This is a short, violent outburst that seems personal. The others contain ramblings of a deeper ideological nature," Stenman explained.

"Crazy people are crazy. Who can tell what's going through their heads? In any event, this is a racist threat."

"Do you have surveillance cameras?" Stenman asked.

"No. We do have an alarm system for the indoor premises, though."

I launched a sneak attack. "How is the company doing financially?"

Hulkko appeared almost horrified by my blunt question. "I don't understand what that has to do with Jacobson's murder."

"Jacobson's wife told us that the company had taken out a loan from an Estonian finance company to fund the construction of this building. Have there been any problems with the loan?"

"Absolutely not… Some minor delays in payments perhaps, but they've already been settled."

"And yet Jacobson planned on transferring the loan to a Finnish bank?"

"Yes, he did. Circumstances change. When we originally took out the loan, it was cheaper in Estonia. Now things aren't going as well there, and interest rates at Finnish banks are more affordable. There's nothing more to it than that."

"Was it the father's or the son's idea?"

"Samuel's, but Roni wasn't opposed."

I told Hulkko that Jacobson hadn't been away because of the flu, but because he was afraid of something. Hulkko shook his head in disbelief. "Are you sure?"

"Can you think of anything that would have frightened him so much he didn't dare to set foot outside his home?"

"Nothing except those fanatics. Maybe they've threatened him before. What else could it be?"

"His wife came up with several reasons," I said. "Jacobson could have owed someone money, he could have had an affair and been afraid of the woman's husband, he could have gotten mixed up in criminal activity..."

"Ethel has an active imagination. In matters like those, Samuel was as conventional as they come. There was no way he had anything to do with criminals or other men's wives. He would have run in the other direction if a woman had approached him with those kinds of intentions. He was absolutely faithful."

Absolutely faithful, I thought. I had no trouble at all imagining Samuel Jacobson succumbing if faced with irresistible temptation.

"Still, isn't it understandable that his wife imagined all kinds of things because her husband refused to tell her what was going on?"

"Could be, but I still find it pretty incredible."

"How long have you worked for Jacobson?"

"Almost twenty years."

"Were you two on good terms?"

"There's no other way I would have stayed here so long. This has been a good place to work, always has been. They look out for their employees."

Stenman found this odd. "And yet he didn't give you even the slightest hint as to the nature of his fears?"

"Samuel was private when it came to his personal affairs. And it's not as if I were his best friend."

"Who was, then?"

"I'm not sure, but I'm guessing you'll find whomever it is at the synagogue. Samuel was a very active member of the congregation in recent years. He belonged to the board of trustees. He was so proud when he was elected that he brought in cake for the entire staff. Once, when we were alone, he told me that it was only now that he was older that he felt any affinity for the Israeli cause... I heard that he wrote some harsh things in the congregation newsletter about the Palestinian situation and Arabs. He even showed me one of the pieces, and it was pretty provocative. Maybe that set someone off."

"Maybe. How many people work here?"

"About twenty. We were almost half again as many in the '80s, since the repair and maintenance department was so big, but computers changed that, too."

Stenman stepped in. "Has there been any tension inside the company? Have you had to let employees go, for instance?"

"We've been hit by the recession just like everyone else, but luckily we haven't had to resort to lay-offs yet. Samuel believes that a company should take care of its own, even when things aren't going well. Roni and I suggested that four employees be offered an early retirement package, but he wouldn't hear of it, because the employees wanted to stay on."

"What about any lay-offs for reasons other than the recession?"

"There was one. An unfortunate case."

"When did it happen?"

"A couple of months ago, give or take."

Stenman wanted more. "What happened?"

"Drinking on the job. A shame. He was a good employee."

A thought occurred to me. "Could you please ask all the employees that are here today to gather together? I'd like to say a few words to them."

"Now?"

"Yes. Before that, I want to have a look inside the safe. Jacobson's wife gave me the keys."

Hulkko told the secretary to call the staff together. In the meantime, I examined the safe, which was in the CEO's office. It contained cash reserves of five thousand euros, a cheque-book and a packet of lunch vouchers.

Ten minutes later, all of the employees were in the conference room except the driver, who was out on his rounds. There wasn't enough room for everyone to sit. I stood at the head of the table and surveyed the crowd, which was eyeing me inquisitively.

"I'm Detective Kafka from the Helsinki Police, and this is my colleague, Detective Stenman. We're investigating the murder of your employer, Samuel Jacobson. We're trying to find a motive for the crime. Discovering it is critical to our investigation. I know from experience that motives can be surprising. It could be something that happened years ago; it could be hate, love, jealousy, money, racism, revenge. It might be related to work or free time. We know that Jacobson had stayed home from work for three days because he was afraid of something, but we don't know what. I'm hoping you all can help me. He may have told someone something, or one of you may have heard or seen something that can help us make progress in the investigation. So if you know something, you can either tell us now or contact us later. We'll leave our phone numbers on the bulletin board."

The silence lasted at least twenty seconds.

"I'm curious about the letter that was found in the mail box this morning," said a balding man in his fifties. From his mustard-coloured coat, I deduced he worked in maintenance.

"We're looking into it and any possible connection to Jacobson's murder, but for the moment we can't tell you any more than that. So let's agree that we ask the questions, you just tell us if you know something."

Another twenty seconds of silence. Then a young guy standing in the doorway raised his hand, like a kid asking for permission to answer a teacher's question.

"Yes?"

"I don't know if this has anything to do with it, but a couple of weeks ago the boss asked me to check the security and fire-wall on his home computer. He suspected that someone had hacked into it and installed spyware. I didn't find anything, but I was pretty sure someone had got into it. They had just done a good job cleaning up after themselves, so I couldn't tell who it was and if anything had happened. I updated the virus software and scanned the computer."

The guy seemed out of breath after his high-speed mono-logue.

"Did Jacobson say why he suspected someone had got into his computer?"

"He just said that he had read somewhere how easy it was to break into computers and wanted to make sure that the competitors didn't know anything about the company's bids and stuff. It sounded a little strange coming out of the blue like that, but I still did what he asked me to."

"When you say Jacobson's home computer, are you refer-ring to his laptop?"

"Yes."

"What do you mean that you were pretty sure someone had got into it?"

"Files had been copied from his computer in the middle of the night. I asked Jacobson if he had been using his computer then, and he said no."

"What files?"

"Email, at least."

"Did Jacobson have any ideas as to who the infiltrator might have been?" Stenman asked.

"No."

"Did he ever mention it again?"

"No. It didn't go any further than that."

I thanked him and asked if anyone had anything else to report, but everyone just stood there, exchanging glances in silence.

"Thank you. You can get back to work."

Before we left, I went over to the bulletin board and pinned up my number, Stenman's number and our unit's twenty-four-hour number.

"This is a pretty unusual case," Stenman said, once we were outside. I admitted it was.

"Why didn't Jacobson contact the police if he was too scared to even leave the house?" she wondered.

"Because he was mixed up in something he couldn't tell the police about."

"That's what I was thinking. And that threat letter is another wrinkle."

"You think it's a ruse to get us to believe that the killer is a racist?"

Stenman chuckled. "Yes, don't you?"

"Yes. The timing was too convenient – right before the murder – and it really isn't even close to the other ones."

I scanned the vicinity. Across the road there was a metalworks, up and over to the right a car dealership squeezed in behind a chain-link fence, and to the left a plastics and rubber wholesaler.

"While we're here, let's have a look and see if there are any surveillance cameras in the area."

We started from the rubber company. Apparently rubber wasn't of much interest to thieves, because we didn't find a camera. The car dealership, on the other hand, produced results. The camera was on the wall of the hut that contained the office. It was positioned to monitor the used cars standing three-deep in the fenced lot, which meant it was aimed right at the road.

Stenman turned into the lot and pulled up next to the hut. The salesman came out before we had a chance to open our doors. The recession was so bad even car dealers were picking up the pace.

"Hi there. What kind of car are you looking for?"

I showed the salesman my police badge, and introduced us. He looked openly disappointed.

I indicated to the camera. "Is that surveillance camera in operation?"

"That's the idea."

"Show us how it works."

We followed the salesman in. The hut was hot and smelt of coffee that had been standing too long. A rack filled with car keys hung on the wall. A copier and a printer occupied one corner, and a computer and the surveillance camera monitor stood on the desk.

"I can use this control here to aim and zoom the camera. When I go home at night, I start recording. It goes to this hard drive. If nothing out of the ordinary happens, I empty the hard drive once a week."

"Show us how wide an area the camera captures."

The dealer's curiosity was now clearly piqued. "What is it you're looking for?"

I didn't answer; I just told him to play the recording. He fiddled with the machine for a while, and finally got it to work. The guy was no technological prodigy.

"So this is from this morning."

Stenman and I watched the image intently. The clock was running at the bottom of the screen; the footage was from 8 a.m. It was already light, and we had no problem making out the road between the gaps in the rows of cars – or the left corner of Jacobson's business and the mail box standing there. A van entered from the right and disappeared to the left.

"Looks good. I'm interested in the period between yesterday evening and eight o' clock this morning. Can you copy the last ten hours onto a DVD or something?"

"That's gonna take a heck of a lot of time."

"Then it's probably best if we take the hard drive back to headquarters and go through it at our leisure."

"Don't you need some sort of permission slip for that?"

"Do you have some reason to not show that recording to the police?"

"Of course not," he said. "When would I get it back?"

"Tomorrow at the latest."

"Oh, go ahead and take it, then. It's never been any use anyway."

4

Investigating murders is usually simple, which is why the percentage of cases solved is high. The killer often leaves behind traces, or else traces of the victim are left behind on the killer. Also, the murderer is usually found among those close to the victim, and the motive is almost always easy to deduce. In Finnish murders, it is jealousy, money, a grudge, booze.

If the motive remains unclear, the investigation is immediately trickier. If, in addition, the perpetrator and the victim aren't acquainted, the investigation grows even more complicated. And there's a third factor that can hamper an investigation: if the perpetrator is a professional, or at least intelligent and careful.

Jacobson's murder fit all of the criteria of a difficult case. Talking to the neighbours hadn't produced any results. No one had seen the Golf, or anything else that would have furthered the investigation. The murderer's getaway route also remained unclear. A car coming from the scene of the crime could only access the more open waters of Tammisalo by one of two routes: down Tammisalontie and past the manor towards Herttoniemi, or down Ruonasalmentie towards Roihuvuori. There were no surveillance cameras along there, either. After that, the number of alternatives increased dramatically.

The make of the getaway car had been released to the radio stations, television channels and papers that afternoon, but it hadn't made any difference. Not a single clue had come in, even though the murder made the prime-time broadcast. A car as common as a Golf didn't attract any attention. No one had seen a driver dressed like a police officer, either. Presumably the murderer had changed clothes, or at least covered his police uniform with a coat.

I ordered Stenman to review the footage, and Simolin to call through all of the car rental agencies in town; the call data from Jacobson's landline and his cell phone had already been requested. The Golf was not a phantom car, after all; it was steel, aluminium and plastic. An owner would turn up if we just looked long enough. Dejected, I dropped by Huovinen's office to report the latest on the investigation and went downstairs to eat. I had just started eating my soup when my phone rang. I didn't recognize the number.

"Auvinen here. I'm the driver, and I was just out taking care of some deliveries when you dropped by the company. I heard you were looking for information, all kinds of information about the boss. I have something to tell you…"

I found a pen but no paper. I grabbed the tabloid from the neighbouring table; it would have to serve as an impromptu notebook.

"Yeah?"

"This happened about three weeks ago. The boss's car was in the shop and he asked for a ride to a client meeting in Vantaa. Someone called him during the drive. I wasn't trying to eavesdrop, but he sounded afraid, so my ears just sort of pricked up."

"What was he talking about?"

"I was just coming to that. At first he said that he didn't want to be, or couldn't, get involved in anything… He didn't say anything in greater detail about what. The caller talked for a long time, and then the boss started almost shouting that he wasn't going to cooperate in any way, shape or form. The caller talked some more, and when it was the boss's turn to speak, he said that no company is that important and that he – the caller, I mean – could do whatever he wanted but that he was not going to be involved. Then he hung up."

"Did he explain the call in any way?"

"Not a word. He was quiet for the rest of the trip; he was clearly thinking about something."

"Do you remember the exact date?"

"Tuesday. It was the third. Check the phone data and you'll find out who it was who called. I have a hunch it could be the killer. The boss was afraid of him, at least."

"Does anything else come to mind?"

"Nope, that's it."

"What was your opinion of Jacobson?"

"In what sense?"

"Overall impression. What was he like?"

"A stubborn old bird, but otherwise a nice guy. On a pretty different wavelength from Jacobson junior."

"Are you saying they fought a lot?"

"Not a lot, but sometimes. The son wanted to establish a subsidiary in Tallinn, but the boss thought it was too risky."

"What about others? Did Jacobson have disagreements with anyone else?"

"No."

"Not even Hulkko?"

"Nah, Hulkko is an even-keeled guy."

"Could Jacobson have been involved with a woman?"

Auvinen laughed. "Not a chance. He was terrified of women."

"What do you think about the threat that turned up this morning? Did you hear about that?"

"Yeah. There are all kinds of nut jobs on the loose, but it didn't seem like much."

I thanked Auvinen and asked him to call if he thought of anything else. I never finished my soup. I headed right up to Stenman's office, where she was watching the security tape fast-forwarded many times the normal speed.

"How's it going?"

"I'm already at 6 a.m. I've noted the times of any vehicles that have driven past, plus the make if I recognize it. No Golfs so far. I can't make out the licence plates because the camera is filming straight from the side. It was a quiet night. Only a few cars drove past, and some of those were patrol cars or security company vehicles."

"Well, if we don't get anything else, maybe at least we'll get the time... Can you stay late tonight?"

"I'm in no rush. The boys will be fine by themselves."

Both of Stenman's sons were over ten years old, and she had a mother in good health who lived nearby and was willing to watch them.

I told her about the call I had just received from Auvinen. "It sounds like Jacobson was hiding from whoever it was. I'll ask Simolin to trace the call."

Stenman was doubtful. "It's probably one of those prepaid numbers."

Simolin walked in, carrying a notebook. "I've checked with all of the rental agencies in the Helsinki area. It's not a rental."

"No cars have been reported stolen, it hasn't been rented, and chances are it's not the killer's own car. What alternatives do we have left?" I pondered.

"Borrowed," Simolin suggested.

"Professionals don't borrow cars. Too big a risk," Stenman said.

"Borrowed without permission, from some company or by blackmailing the owner."

"Possible, but that's also risky, unless the killer has the owner of the car in a serious vice. What if the car was stolen from someone who couldn't report it, like long-term airport parking? The owner might be abroad."

"The new Golfs are equipped with immobilizers, and there are surveillance cameras at the parking lots. I just had an idea. What if the car is foreign, say Estonian? You can buy cars there without ID; you can make up any name you want. There's no way to connect the buyer to the car."

"It's possible," I said. "The important thing now is to find that car. It was already on the news, but we've got to get it into the papers, too. Find a photo of a similar Golf somewhere and ask the papers to print it. Not everyone knows what a Golf looks like – at least, not all women do."

"Come and take a look at this," Stenman said.

She rewound the recording and pressed Play. The footage showed a car, irritatingly at the far right of the screen, pulling up in front of Jacobson's company. A man who appeared drunk climbed out. He looked around nervously, hurried over to the mail box, and slipped in an object that looked like a letter. The time on the screen read 6:32 a.m.

Even in still mode the image was so grainy and blurry that there was no way of identifying the guy. Stenman wound it back and forth a few times, but it didn't do any good. The clothes were normal; they didn't have any logos. Then Stenman fast-forwarded.

"Oh, for Christ's sakes," Stenman said. The car backed away and disappeared for good.

Simolin provided the play-by-play: "Turned around by backing up in the drive."

"We're not going to get the car or the guy from that," I said, exasperated. You could only see a foot of the car's nose, and even that was caught in an annoying shadow that fell across the front grille. You couldn't even tell what colour it was, just that it was dark.

"Shitty luck, nothing we can do," Stenman said.

"What about Oksanen?" Simolin suggested.

"What about him?"

"He came in second in the *Tech World* car identification competition a couple of years back. I just saw him in his office, even though he's supposed to be on vacation."

"Ask him to come in here," I said.

As we waited on Oksanen's expertise, Stenman rewound and fast-forwarded through the footage a few more times and fine-tuned it. Then Simolin walked in with Oksanen.

"What's the trouble?" Oksanen asked confidently. Simolin must have given him the low-down.

"Do you recognize that car?" Stenman asked.

Oksanen bent towards the screen and, without a moment's hesitation, said: "Late '90s Ford Mondeo. The last year they made them was '97, if I remember right. Piece of cake."

I was blown away. "Are you sure?"

"This is one of the easiest models to identify. The newer ones would be a lot tougher. See how the headlight curves in from the edges in that weird way?"

"Great," I said, instinctively slapping Oksanen on the shoulder. He took it as praise, and exited with a smile on his face.

Simolin's phone rang. I continued talking to Stenman: "Let's ask Hulkko and the other employees about the car..."

The eagerness in Simolin's voice caught my attention. I looked over and saw him lift up a thumb.

"No, tell me... where is it...?" Simolin wrote something down. "Good, I'll go over right now and have a look. Call in forensics and a tow truck, too."

I guessed what had happened. Simolin ended the call and confirmed my suspicions.

"We have our Golf."

5

I was forced to admit that Jacobson's killer was not your average criminal. He had left the car only a hundred yards from the scene of the murder. It was discovered in the garage of the house that was across the street and up from the Jacobsons', the beautiful old run-down house that Jacobson's neighbour had mentioned. The trees and bushes had blocked him from seeing that the car had been driven there.

From up close, the house was in even worse shape than I had imagined. It was a two-storey villa, with a glassed-in porch and steep-pitched roofs. The paint was flaking and the roof tiles were green with moss, but even the ravages of time couldn't mask its beauty. That beauty wasn't likely to keep the heirs from tearing it down, however. Money steamrolled over sentiment, too. Still, at least three generations had lived in the house, and even those who remained had started life there.

The garden was overgrown, as if no one mowed or pruned it any more. Saplings and grass, almost waist high, thrust up through the gravel drive. The ground under the fruit trees was blanketed with rotting apples of all varieties that would never find their way into a jam jar or juice bottle in anyone's cellar. The air was laden with end-of-summer abundance.

The gravel crunched under our feet as we walked up the slope towards the house. Two patrol cars stood in the drive.

The yard had been searched and all the footprints pulled before our arrival. The car was waiting to be towed to the technical facility for a detailed forensic investigation.

"It's gorgeous here," Stenman sighed.

"It sure is."

The Golf had been driven into a weatherboard garage that stood between the house and the upper yard. Its double doors were open, and I could see the rear of the vehicle.

"How did the killer know about the garage?" Simolin wondered. "What if he's a local?"

"Maybe he just came and checked out the area beforehand."

"The garage lock is smashed," Stenman said, peering in through the car windows.

The car had been found by some neighbourhood boys who had been in the yard stealing plums. They had carried out these raids before, and had always been able to go about their business without anyone bothering them. This time, the car in the garage had scared them. Luckily for us, one of the boys heard at home that there had been a murder across the street and that the police were looking for a blue Volkswagen Golf. The boy's mother called it in, and a patrol drove out to make sure that the car was the one we were looking for.

I hung back to speak with one of the forensic specialists.

"The plates are from a demolished vehicle," she said.

"Anything else?"

"There's a policeman's jacket and hat in the back seat. We'll conduct a more detailed investigation at the impound facility in Pasila."

Stenman circled the car. "Can I take a look inside?"

"As long as you don't mess up the prints."

"I won't," she promised, pulling on a pair of rubber gloves. I watched as she bent into the car from the passenger door. She had a nice butt, and my eyes automatically honed in on it. But I was forced to break the spell and focus on the situation at hand.

"Did you find any footprints or anything else in the yard?" I asked the investigators.

"Nothing. The ground's hard and didn't take any prints."

Stenman rose from the car and said: "It looks like the car was brought over from Estonia."

"What makes you think that?"

"Come and have a look."

Stenman opened the glove box. A sticker from a Tallinn car dealership was pasted to the inside of the hatch.

"That's no good. Might be hard to find out who the owner is."

Simolin, who had circled the house, walked over carrying an apple.

"These are good," he said, juice spurting as he bit.

"You were right – the car was probably brought from Estonia."

"That might still turn to our advantage," Simolin said, opening the hood. He wrote down the engine number and stepped off to the side. I saw him make a call.

I took a closer look at the car. There was a police officer's coat and hat in the back seat, along with a removable blue light for the roof.

"At least there's no doubt that we have the right car," I said to Stenman. "I'm having a hard time deciding whether it was smart or stupid to leave the car this close to the scene."

"Smart," Stenman said. "A path leads from the top of the hill down to a bigger road. The killer probably had a second car waiting there. He must have assumed that it wouldn't take long before someone noticed the murder and an APB would be put out on the Golf. With the second car, he could drive around without having to worry, since everyone was looking for the wrong make."

Simolin walked over, looking satisfied with himself. Normally he was modesty personified.

"I called a detective I know in Tallinn. He promised to try and see if there was anything he could find out about the vehicle."

"How do you know him?" Stenman asked.

Simolin looked embarrassed. "We share some common interests."

"Is he into Indians, too?"

"Something like that."

"Maybe I should start getting into them, too," Stenman said. She looked like she was serious. I had never heard her make fun at the expense of Simolin's pastime. On the contrary, she had praised him to me on numerous occasions.

"In any case, everything points to the theory that the killer is a professional," I said. "It was all carefully planned, down to the acquisition of the vehicle. It looks like the threat letter that Jacobson received doesn't have anything to do with the murder. It's not likely that the killer would have used two cars on the same day. If he wanted us to connect the threat and the murder, he would have only used the Golf."

Stenman was satisfied. "At least that's one less alternative."

I climbed the path that started behind the house and rose to the top of the hill. I looked around. The trail dropped through a small stand of trees and plunged down to the narrow, spruce-lined road. I returned to the yard just as the tow truck was grinding its way up the drive. The forensic investigators were pushing the car out of the garage with the help of a couple of patrolmen. Once they got it out, they turned it around so it could be winched onto the bed of the truck.

"If we're lucky, we'll find something in the car that will help us with the investigation," Simolin said.

I didn't believe in luck. It wasn't likely that the killer would have made such an elementary mistake.

"We need to talk to the people who live on the road that starts on the far side of that hill. They might have noticed the killer's other car. It was probably parked there overnight."

"I'm on it," Simolin said. Stenman nodded, too.

Simolin's phone rang. He glanced at it and said: "It's Estonia." Stenman and I stopped to listen.

"Wait, let me write that down."

I handed Simolin a pen and a notebook.

"All right, go for it," he said, jotting down the information he was getting. "Thanks a lot; I owe you one."

Simolin frowned at the notebook. "The car was sold by a legitimate importer a little over a year ago. It's owned by an Estonian finance company, which is also the registered user. It was stolen from the company's parking garage two weeks ago."

I had a sinking feeling. "What's the name of the company?" I asked. Simolin took another glance at his notebook.

"Baltic Invest."

6

Roni Jacobson's plane from Rovaniemi was landing at 7:15 p.m., and it would take about twenty minutes for the bags to come through. Stenman and I waited in the short-stay lot. I was tired, and I rolled down the window to get some fresh air.

"How well do you know Jacobson's son?" Stenman asked.

"Not well. We haven't seen each other in years. The last time was in passing, at some community event."

"I always thought all the Jews in Finland fraternized with each other."

"I'm an exception," I said, sounding stuck-up even to myself.

Stenman smiled. "Why don't you go to the synagogue and find yourself a nice Jewish girl, get married under the canopy, and smash a wine glass under your heel. I've seen *Fiddler on the Roof*."

"I know all the nice Jewish girls in Finland, and they're already married. And if I married a Finnish Jew, I'd be marrying her entire family. Just the thought gives me the willies."

I was telling the truth, but I still shouldn't have said anything to Stenman.

"I thought family was the only thing that mattered to Jews?"

"For some it is, for others it's not. Most of us marry outside the faith."

"Isn't that a shame?"

"It's pretty natural. What would be weird would be if people from as small a group as us Jews only bred... only married each other."

Stenman had been my subordinate for years, but she had

never asked about my Jewishness before. Maybe she felt that prying was indelicate.

I saw Roni Jacobson exit the terminal carrying a bulging gym bag in one hand and a fishing rod case in the other.

I got out of the car; Stenman followed. Roni saw me, and we shook hands. He had aged since the last time we had met. Despite the fact that he was a couple of years younger than me, he was already greying, and he had a bald spot the size of an apple at the crown of his head. A few days of stubble covered his chin.

I had never particularly liked Roni. Ever since he was a kid there had been an air of arrogance about him, and character traits like that don't just disappear. One glance at Roni's face was enough to see that things hadn't changed – at least not for the better.

"I'm sorry for your loss," I said. "This here is Detective Stenman."

"Mom's waiting, so… Are we going to stand here, or should we get in the car?"

"We can give you a lift and talk during the ride. We'll do the official interrogation sometime later."

I opened the trunk. Roni dropped in his luggage and joined me in the back seat. Stenman drove.

"Did you catch anything?" I asked.

Roni's tone was impatient. "A couple of trout and some grayling."

We chatted for a minute about Lapland: the weather, the night frosts, the autumn colours. As we curved onto Ring Road III, Roni said: "What was it you wanted to ask me about?"

"Your father was afraid of something. He had stayed home from work for three days because of it. Did he discuss it with you?"

"Yeah, that's what Mom said. At first I thought he was just sick. I wouldn't have gone to Lapland if I had known… It wasn't until Mom called that I found out that something else was going on, but Dad wouldn't say what."

"When did you leave for Lapland?"

"Four days ago. The company owns a cabin at Pyhä. I always go up fishing there this time of year with a couple of buddies. I didn't see any reason to make an exception this year, because I hadn't taken my vacation yet and there was nothing special going on at the office."

"Was the timing of the trip your idea or your father's?"

"Mine, because it had to work for my friends too. But I discussed it with Dad, of course. He was fine with it."

Roni's phone rang. "It's Mom."

"Feel free to answer."

Roni took the call and talked with Ethel for a second.

"… I have to get off. I'll be there in just a minute."

Once the call ended, I pressed on. "There must be a good reason for your father's murder. Do you have any idea what it might be?"

"Isn't it obvious? Anti-Semitism. I heard he got a threatening letter at work."

"Yes, we heard about that, too, and went and met with your staff. We don't believe that the letter has anything to do with the murder."

"What do you mean?"

"We have our own information, but we can't discuss it yet."

"In that case I have no idea…" Roni looked disappointed. Evidently anti-Semitism would have been an agreeable motive for the murder. Anything else meant complications.

"The perpetrator was very methodical. That implies that the motive was not something random. Could the firm's finances have anything to do with the crime?"

"I don't know what you're talking about. We're in a bit of a tight spot at the moment, like thousands of other companies, but it's nothing more than that. Our debt load is relatively low compared to our assets and net worth."

"Your father wanted to take out a new loan in Finland and pay off the Estonian loan. Why?"

"It was some bee he got in his bonnet. We couldn't have got a loan any more cheaply here than from Estonia."

"So you were opposed?"

"It would have been six of one, half a dozen of the other."

"How did you end up taking a loan from Estonia in the first place?"

"We received an offer when we started planning construction of the new building."

"From whom?"

"Max Oxbaum. I happened to mention to him at some event that Dad wanted to build new offices for the company. Max said that he represented an Estonian finance company and could arrange a loan. It was all above board."

"Were you opposed to the construction project?"

"No. It seemed like a good idea at the time. I might feel differently now. But no one else predicted the recession, either."

"Could your father have taken out another loan under the table?"

"Not a chance. And why would he?"

"Say, some personal reason, and then maybe he left the loan unpaid?"

"No," Roni snapped. "Like I said, the company and Dad had assets. Why wouldn't he have realized his assets instead? I'm pretty sure most people would rather pay a debt than die."

"You'd think so."

We stopped at a traffic light. Stenman glanced back. "When did your father intend to retire?"

"By sixty-four at the latest, in other words a little under two years from now."

"Was he in good health?"

"Sure. He was a little overweight and had high blood pressure, but otherwise he was healthy. What does this have to do with Dad's murder?"

"Did he have life insurance?"

Now Roni was upset. "Yes, and Mom's the beneficiary. You guys can't be turning this into insurance fraud."

I tried to calm him down and explain that the police have to ask unpleasant questions. My reassurances didn't have the desired effect.

"Can't we talk about these things later…?"

"Unfortunately not. Did Oxbaum handle all the loan arrangements himself, or did you meet representatives of the lender?"

"I didn't meet anyone but Oxbaum."

"But I assume you looked into the finance company, to see if it was solid?"

"No. Dad might have, through his contacts in Israel. He told me that he trusted Max… Besides, it's your brother's company, too," Roni gloated, as if he had found a weapon to use against me.

"Does the name Benjamin Hararin mean anything to you?"

"No."

"What about Amos Jakov?"

"You mean the Israeli billionaire?"

"Yes."

"Well, that's about the extent of my knowledge. He's an Israeli billionaire. What does he have to do with this? It sounds like you guys are letting this case get the better of your imaginations —"

"He and Hararin own the finance company Max was representing."

"So? They're way off in Israel and we're here. Are you finding some significant connections between the two?" Roni asked sharply.

Stenman pulled up in front of the Jacobsons' house.

"You can go. We'll be in touch."

Once Roni had stepped through the gate, I asked Stenman, "What do you think?"

"I didn't like him, but that's not what you asked."

"Roni has always thrown money around. When he was twenty,

he drove a Porsche, and he also had a big boat. Sort of a minor-league jet-setter. I heard that a year or so ago he moved into a new place in Marjaniemi: 3,000 square feet, sea views."

"What if this is about the son's spending, not the father's, and Pops just ended up footing the bill? Maybe Roni had been given his final warning and he hightailed it off to Lapland. He asked the old man not to leave the house."

"He couldn't have stayed away forever."

"Maybe he was trying to drum up money to pay off his debts in the meantime."

"Roni said that his Dad was going to stay on as CEO until he turned sixty-four, so well over a year from now. According to Ethel, Samuel had planned on retiring earlier. Samuel had told his neighbours the end of this year. Sounds like Samuel had decided to push back his retirement. Roni probably wasn't too thrilled about that."

"Still, it's not likely he'd kill his Dad... What was all that about Hararin and Jakov?" Stenman asked.

"Don't worry about that yet."

Stenman eyed me evaluatively. Roni's gibe about my brother hadn't gone unnoticed. "All right, I won't worry about that... yet. Is Roni Jacobson a family man?"

"Two children from a previous marriage, and one from the new one."

"Wouldn't it have made more sense to send muscle to threaten his family instead of his father?"

"Maybe the person making the threats figured that the old man was the one with the money. He doesn't care who pays, as long as he gets his dough."

"Should we take a closer look at the company's finances, and the son's, too?" Stenman asked. "Maybe it's worth having another word with CFO Pekka Hulkko."

I couldn't have agreed more.

7

I got to my one-bedroom apartment in Punavuori around 9 p.m. and was greeted by the fug of loneliness that clings to every bachelor pad. I had a reputation of sorts as a ladies' man, although I didn't get where it came from. Maybe I was paying for my years of youthful experimentation and unsavoury stories were being passed from one Jewish family to the next as a cautionary example. The fact was that it had been over six years since I had last lived with a woman. At the time, I had been in a relationship with a Finnish teacher named Suvi whom I had met at a colleague's wedding. I still wasn't sure why the relationship had ended, but apparently the blame was mine.

Living alone had its advantages, but it wasn't a dogma or principle for me. It was ninety per cent sad, especially when your wildest partying days had passed and you started valuing other things.

I don't know what my problem was, but I attracted the wrong sort of women. They represented one of two extremes: either they were too bossy and domineering, or too meek and adaptable.

Another problem was that all the women my age were divorced and usually bitter about it. Plus they had children, and even though I had met some nice kids, I didn't want to be a father to the children of a man I didn't know.

As a bachelor over the age of forty, my relatives considered me a strange bird. I was continuously dodging their attempts to marry me off. "Good Jewish girls" were foisted off on me under any variety of pretences.

I may not be qualified to comment, but I think women found me pretty interesting, and pretty good-looking, too. Something in my melancholic disposition aroused their protective instincts. Plus I kept myself in shape, owned a place in a good neighbourhood, and had a respectable job. I should have been a good match, but I just wasn't able to sell myself to anyone.

I shook myself out of my gloomy musings, popped open a beer and wondered what I should do about Eli. I eventually made my decision and called him. We used to get together at least once a week, but now it had been three weeks since we had last seen each other. We must have overdosed on each other's company at the cottage.

Eli was the first to speak. "What's up, little brother?" I knew him well enough to tell he was drunk – not very, but still.

"Are you at home?"

"Yeah, I'm sipping some pricey vintage whisky. Got it from the father-in-law. What about you?"

"I need to talk to you about something."

"Is it about Jacobson? I heard someone shot him."

I wasn't the least bit surprised Eli knew about the case. He was on the executive council of the congregation, just like Jacobson, and even if he hadn't been, he still would have heard about it. Someone called someone else, and that someone called a third person. Two hours later, half the Jews in Helsinki knew about it. We had always been good at disseminating information.

"Are you investigating?"

"Yup. Why would you think I'd be interested in discussing Jacobson with you, of all people?"

"Because I know him and —"

"You have time to meet?"

"There's plenty in this bottle for the both of us. Come over and join me."

"No thanks. Half an hour, at the shore?"

"At the same old spot?"

*

The same old spot was the Compass Terrace at Kaivopuisto marina. When we were kids, Dad would take us down to the shore and regale us with all sorts of stories about the city. At one point, we had an old wooden fisherman's boat, and it had been moored down at the marina, too. An autumn gale had smashed the hull, and it sank a day before Dad was supposed to pull it out for the winter. We never went out in it, because Dad didn't trust the engine, but we'd often take day trips down to the dock. We'd sit in the boat and fish, and Dad would cook for us on a camp stove. We even spent the night a couple of times. I'll always remember the smell of diesel and damp wood that rose from the engine and the bilge.

Eli only lived a couple of hundred yards from our meeting place, but I wouldn't have been surprised if he had shown up in his car. He came on foot, though, and as if by tacit agreement, we headed down the shore towards Cafe Ursula.

Eli broke the silence. "You dated Jacobson's daughter for a while, didn't you? Wasn't her name Lea?"

"You have a good memory."

"It's a small world."

"Smaller than you'd think. Jacobson's wife told me that they took out a loan for their company through you and Max."

Eli shrugged. "Could be. Max handles that side of the business. Besides, you're talking as if we're a bank. All we do is refer clients to the finance company and receive a certain compensation for that. It's not enough to get rich off."

"Where does the money come from?"

"A lot of places. The company I represent has operations in numerous countries. Do you think we have something to do with Jacobson's death? Is that the reason for this clandestine rendezvous?"

"Well, do you?"

"Hey, don't joke around about serious stuff. What the hell is going on here, little brother?"

Even though Eli was trying to keep the tone light, I could sense the fear in him.

"Jacobson wasn't killed by some neo-Nazi or crazy racist. The killer was dressed like a police officer because Jacobson knew that something might happen to him. He had barricaded himself up at home. He was frightened. And he wouldn't tell anyone why, even his wife."

"What reason would anyone have to murder a guy who sells office machines?"

"Depends on whether he was just a guy who sold office machines. Or something more."

"A spy?" Eli chuckled. "It's hard to imagine anyone more strait-laced than Jacobson. People like that don't get mixed up in anything dangerous."

"What were the terms of the loan like?"

"What you're asking is confidential information."

"I doubt Jacobson's very concerned any more."

"Who would take a loan from us if the terms weren't good?"

"What about collateral?"

"Totally normal. Corporate real estate and the house."

"So why did Jacobson want to switch banks if everything was so good?"

Eli slowed down and looked at me. "I don't know anything about that. Where did you hear that?"

"His wife."

"I seriously don't know anything about that, but I can ask Max… or you can ask him yourself."

"You didn't tell me anything about the company you represent. What's it called?"

"Baltic Invest. It's an investment and finance company."

"Estonian?"

"No, it's part of a larger international concern."

"Come on, who owns the company?"

"It's part of an Israeli conglomerate. The principal shareholder is a businessman named Benjamin Hararin."

"A Jew."

"What could be finer than the success of one of our own?"

"How did it so happen that you and Max became the company's agents in Finland?"

"Through Max. A friend of his knows Hararin and suggested it to him. I wasn't thrilled about it, but Max felt like free money was being thrown into our laps. All we had to do was introduce potential borrowers and lenders to each other. We'd get a slice of every loan – a slim one, but it wasn't much work. Once Max filled out the papers for a million-euro loan in fifteen minutes. We got 20,000 euros for that. Pretty good hourly rate."

"Does the name Amos Jakov say anything to you?"

"What you're trying to insinuate isn't true," Eli said. He was starting to get angry.

"What is it I'm trying to insinuate?"

"I know what's been written about Jakov in Israel. That Hararin is his frontman and launders Russian mafia money for him. The police there have been investigating it for years, but they haven't found any proof."

"If my brother says so, it must be true. How much have you guys brokered in loans?"

"We have several hundred clients, and they have a total of sixty million in loans. Jacobson was one of them."

I did some quick mental calculations. If Max and Eli earned a similar slice for each loan, they had raked in 1.2 million euros from them. Not bad, considering that the business had only been in existence for a couple of years. Two men of modest needs would have no trouble living off that.

"How did he know to turn specifically to you and Max for a loan?"

Eli was genuinely irritated. "Max, again. Although you'd never guess it, he's pretty agile when he wants to be. It'd be nice to know by what logic you're trying to connect us to Jacobson's murder."

"Money's always a good motive."

"Was Jacobson's company in financial hardship?"

"The wife says no, but maybe she didn't know everything. Maybe you do. Did Jacobson make all his payments on time?"

Eli avoided my gaze. "Come on, spit it out."

"The last few payments were late, because Jacobson's company lost a lot of big orders and clients over a short period of time. We tweaked the payment schedule and everyone was happy. We weren't worried, because Jacobson's corporate and personal assets added up to much more than the amount of the loan, and we have collateral for every single cent."

"Then maybe Jacobson had vices his wife didn't know about."

"Gambling and wild women?"

"The wife said he didn't gamble. I'm not sure about the women."

"Believe me, you can drop that line of investigation. That much I knew about the guy."

"So try and come up with a better one," I said.

"I'd start from something more prosaic. Maybe he had fired someone who decided to take revenge. It happens. You know that motives can be pretty unbelievable sometimes. When I was sitting on the bench in municipal court, I had this one case where a guy had locked his buddy in the sauna and set fire to it – and all because his friend had a better hunting dog than he did. It had kept him awake at night, and eventually it sent him off the deep end."

Eli stopped to eye a new, expensive-looking boat moored at one of the docks. "I was thinking I'd buy a boat. How do you like that one?"

"Knock yourself out, as long as you don't ask me to co-sign. You're old enough to make decisions like that yourself."

"You remember Dad's old wooden boat that sank in that autumn storm?"

I nodded.

"I've always wondered why he never took us out in it," Eli said.

"Because the engine was a piece of junk."

"That's what Dad said. So why didn't he fix it?"

"Why do you think?"

"That he was afraid something would happen to us and to him – that the boat would capsize and we'd drown. The sea scared him and lured him at the same time. He solved the conundrum by buying the boat and keeping it at the marina. Pretty weird coincidence that he drowned."

"Come on, we had a good time at the dock."

"I'm not saying we didn't, but it could have been fun to take the boat out to some nice little island, drop anchor, fish and spend the night. We could have turned up the stereo and danced butt-naked around the bonfire, drunk off our asses."

I had no problem imagining Eli at the helm in a captain's hat and a navy-blue Polo cardigan. Imagining him dancing naked around a bonfire was harder, but not impossible. Sometimes he would get seriously blitzed. One night that week at his cottage, he had sat at the shore singing "Jambalaya" for a good half-hour straight, sounding like a bear with bronchitis. At one point he had mixed up the words and bellowed about "Polish piroshki down the bayou."

If Eli was feeling blue, he'd switch from "Jambalaya" to "The Death of the Farmer's Lass": "Before them lay the bog, rough boards bridged the mire…"

I had listened to "Jambalaya" non-stop until he passed out on the granite boulder. The loyal little brother that I was, I kept sitting there at his side, even after it started to rain. He woke up soaking wet and chilled to the bone.

"Up for a beer at the Sea Horse?" Eli suggested.

"Not tonight. I just got off work an hour ago."

"Have you guys got anything yet?"

"No."

"Well, I won't twist your arm. Some other time."

"We found the killer's car," I said, watching Eli's expression.

"Good. Solve the case."

"It was stolen in Tallinn."

"Pretty clever."

"It was owned by an Estonian investment company called Baltic Invest."

Incredulity played across Eli's face until he realized I was serious. It was clear that this was news to him. "Are you shitting me?"

"They reported it stolen a couple of weeks ago."

"Quite the coincidence. You don't think I have anything to do with it, do you?"

"Hard to imagine that you would. But I have to admit, I don't believe it's a coincidence."

Eli stopped and looked at me, perplexed. "What could Baltic Invest have to do with Jacobson's murder?"

"You told me that he didn't make all of his payments. Maybe the company sent a killer to remind him that they weren't the ones to screw around with."

"Baltic Invest is not Assassination Ltd. And like I said, we have collateral. Jacobson even put up his house. Believe me, it has to be a coincidence," Eli insisted, but he looked like he didn't even believe it himself.

Eli glared at me and I glared at him. Then we parted in opposite directions. After a few yards, I glanced back. Eli was just disappearing behind some bushes, turning into the park. I had the distinct impression that we hadn't seen the last of Eli's business affairs.

I had brought Jacobson's computer home. Ethel had given me the password, so I was able to access both the saved documents and email. The laptop was pretty new and didn't contain many files. Jacobson had written some ordinary business letters, plus a few to his daughter in Israel. I felt like I was breaking the bounds of propriety when I read them, but they didn't contain anything of interest in terms of the investigation. The biggest surprise was that Jacobson was writing his memoirs.

The structure was a straightforward chronology, starting from his youth and approaching the present day. The final entries talked about the 1960s and how he met his future wife. They had been introduced to each other in the lobby of a movie theatre. The name of the film had been *Exodus*.

The style was ponderous and swelled from catalogue-style reportage to sentimental syrup. It was hard to imagine a publisher being interested in it. He was probably writing it for his children and grandchildren.

Jacobson's email correspondence had been brisk, but most of it had to do with the company. I read a few messages that had been sent to clients; they were almost imploring. They appealed to long-lasting business relationships and reminded the clients how conscientiously their wishes had always been taken into consideration. The company must have been doing poorly and Jacobson must have been desperate; there's no other way he ever would have written those emails. He must have been ashamed.

I kept browsing and found an email Jacobson had sent to Roni. It was from a month ago.

Mikkola's dismissal has been on my mind, and my feeling is you acted too hastily and high-handedly. Mikkola has always carried out his duties in an exemplary fashion, and as someone who had been with us for such a long time, he deserved better treatment. In the future, I want you to immediately report any problems to me so that nothing of this sort happens again. I must admit I'm disappointed in your actions.

I met with two of our key clients today and both of them have to postpone their hardware upgrades. All in all, it's starting to look like I'm going to have to put off my retirement. I believe that my connections and experience are too valuable to sacrifice in this financial situation. I hope you're not disappointed, even though I had promised to turn the reins over to you. I'll step down as soon as circumstances allow.

I also discussed the loan with Joel. He sounded almost angry, but I explained that switching the loan over to Finland was best, especially since the Israeli police are investigating the parent company. Joel assured me that it's a matter of internal politics and that everything would be fine. Frankly, I don't know what to believe. He's afraid that transferring the loan will spark a chain reaction in Finland, which I find odd. I tried to put him at ease, and told him I had no intention of announcing my affairs over a loudspeaker. I'm too old to be taking risks, especially since I want to leave you a thriving company, not a string of complications.

Could you please contact him right away and tell him you support my decision. That should calm him down. After all, you two know each other better.

Your father, Samuel

It was clear that the relationship between the father and his son was not unproblematic. Nor was the one between the father-in-law and his son-in-law, Joel Kazan.

8

I almost felt guilty that we hadn't got any further, so I went in to work around 7 a.m. I had given orders that I was to be called if anything important turned up, but I had been allowed to sleep through the night without interruption. Hope springs eternal, though. I was eager to find out if some minor lead had appeared that would advance the case.

The car had been gone over carefully, and plenty of fingerprints, hairs, fibres, even dog hairs, had been pulled from it. All of these offered new possibilities for attacking the case. It wasn't likely that a professional like Jacobson's murderer would leave fingerprints or DNA behind in the car. But you never knew; something might turn up.

Nevertheless, things had gone the way I was afraid they would. The night had brought nothing new. Several tips about the car and shady characters had been called in during the late-night hours, but a couple of the callers were "old friends" of ours whom we didn't take seriously. The rest of the tips were vague to the point of being useless.

Huovinen arrived a little after eight and asked me to bring Simolin and Stenman into his office for a meeting as soon as they came in. Both showed up at about the same time, quarter past eight. They had been working until 9 p.m. Two other investigators had been assigned to the case, but they were out in the field, doing things like talking to people who lived near the spot where the Golf was found.

Huovinen was a good boss. He trusted me, and didn't expect the moon and the stars. All he expected was that everyone do their best. Now he looked at me questioningly, but didn't say anything. He waited for me to start. I reported that the investigation hadn't advanced at all since the previous evening, and that we didn't have any new information. Then I told him about the meeting with Roni, and everything else I knew about him.

"So there's some tension between the father and son," Huovinen said.

"That's what it looks like. Roni was supposed to become CEO, but Jacobson senior decided to stay on for the meantime."

"It's hard to imagine that the son would have anything to do with his father's murder. Or?"

Stenman chimed in. "It wouldn't be the first time. Don't forget the Solhbeck case, where the son ordered a hit on his father to get his inheritance faster."

"OK, keep that possibility open, too."

"Jacobson was also arguing with his son-in-law, Joel Kazan. Kazan works for the company that owns Baltic Invest, and he's somehow involved in the loan business. He got upset when Jacobson announced he was paying off the loan and taking out a replacement loan in Finland. So we're starting to see some logical motives take shape."

"What reason would he have to get upset because his father-in-law wanted to pay off his loan?" Stenman asked.

"He was afraid word would spread and other borrowers would follow suit – that they'd suspect that Jacobson had some inside information from his son-in-law. Or maybe he just saw it as a demonstration of no confidence and took offence."

"At least things are starting to happen. How are you planning on proceeding?"

"We're still trying to piece together the movements of the car… Simolin's been in touch with the Estonian National Bureau of Investigation again and requested further information on the vehicle and the theft."

"My friend at the Estonian police told me that the theft was fishy, because the vehicle had disappeared from a locked garage," Simolin reported. "The explanation was that the building was undergoing a major renovation at the time and there were a lot of construction workers around. The doors had been left open, and the keys were on the receptionist's desk. The idea was that anyone who needed the car could use it. The registration was in the glove box, so no one would have noticed anything at the border."

"Why did your friend think there was something fishy about the loss of the car?" Huovinen asked. "The renovation sounds like a perfectly reasonable explanation to me."

"Because the garage surveillance camera had not been on that particular day. The renovation was also used to explain that, but none of the construction workers admitted to having turned it off, and there wasn't any reason to. The camera's controls were in the same reception area as the key."

"Let's hope the Estonians find out more," Huovinen said.

The ball was in my court again, so I said: "We've asked them to rush the telecommunications data. They promised to get it to us by this afternoon. Even if it doesn't tell us who made the threatening call to Jacobson, the mast data might give us something important."

Huovinen was more doubtful. "The killer seems smart enough to know what kind of information can be gleaned from telecommunications data and has probably taken that into account. We shouldn't rely too much on it. He might even try to throw you off with it."

"We'll take that possibility into consideration."

"If the killer is Estonian, there's a good chance he's back home already."

"Simolin also asked the Estonian NBI if they knew anyone who would be a good match for our case and who happened to be out of the country at the time. We're waiting for them to get back to us. If we go with the assumption that the killer was Estonian, then we have to ask why. Only two alternatives make sense: either a Finn ordered a hit from Estonia, or Jacobson's murder is somehow related to Estonia. In the latter case, the first thing to come to my mind is the fact that Jacobson's company took out a loan from an Estonian lender. The company doesn't have any other connections there."

"Are the Israeli police still investigating the parent company?" Huovinen asked.

"I don't know."

"Can you find out? If you could even get unofficial information on what they think about Baltic Invest, that might also help us come up with a motive for the murder."

"Of course."

I saw Stenman jotting something down in her notebook. She looked at it and said: "According to the CFO, there had been no big problems with the loan payments, meaning there wouldn't have been any reason to strong-arm Jacobson. And generally finance companies send debt collectors after people who owe them money, not killers. A dead man isn't going to be making too many payments."

Huovinen looked at me.

"I asked my brother about the loan. According to him, Jacobson's most recent loan payments were late, but they came to an agreement, and a new payment schedule was drafted."

"Anything new on the murder weapon?"

It was Simolin's turn to share information: "According to the lab, it's a .22 calibre Russian Margolin, probably silencer-equipped. It's a common sharpshooting weapon both here and abroad. Hundreds of thousands have been manufactured. Hundreds, if not thousands, exist in Finland. If you use projectiles slower than the speed of sound, it's quieter than an air gun."

I used to own a Margolin, too. I got it when I graduated from the police academy. I used to shoot quite a bit with it at the Viiki shooting range, but eventually I got bored and sold it to a co-worker.

"Divers searched the sea yesterday along the getaway route. They didn't find anything. The search will continue today."

"Good… Did you get anything from the uniform that was recovered from the Golf?"

"Not genuine. Normal blue nylon overalls with badges cut out of duct tape glued to them. Pretty resourceful, actually. From a few yards away it looks completely authentic."

"I got a call from the Jewish congregation yesterday. What do you think, are there any investigative obstacles that require postponement of the funeral?" Huovinen asked me.

"No, no obstacles."

"Well, then you can give their burial society permission to pick up the body. Will you be attending the funeral, by the way?"

"I was planning on it."

"When is it?"

"Tomorrow morning, probably. The daughter's flight from Israel doesn't arrive until tonight."

"Be sure to talk to her, too," Huovinen reminded me.

Stenman's phone rang. She glanced at the number and said: "It's the CFO, Pekka Hulkko. I'll put it on speakerphone."

Everyone quietened down to listen.

"You asked me to ask if any of the employees own a dark, possibly green, old-model Ford Mondeo. The answer is no, but one of our employees knew that Kari Mikkola owns a car like that."

"Who's Kari Mikkola?"

"That employee we talked about, the one who was fired for drinking on the job. One of the other employees said that he bumped into Mikkola in the Citymarket parking lot at Itäkeskus Mall. Mikkola had been driving a dark-green Mondeo with a picture of a dog in the back window. One plus one is often two."

Stenman agreed that that was so. "Did Mikkola have any other run-ins with Jacobson?"

"Which one, father or son?"

"Mostly the father, but the son will do, too."

"As far as I'm aware there was no bad blood between Samuel and Mikkola, but something about Roni rubbed him the wrong way. At least, Mikkola cursed Roni out on his last day on the job. Intoxication may have played a part, of course."

"Did he make any threats?"

"No. If I recall correctly, he used the words 'cocksucking candy-ass scumbag'. I have Mikkola's address if you want it…"

Stenman thanked him and wrote down the address. Mikkola lived in Vantaa.

"Why don't we go have a look? We don't really have anything else going on," Stenman suggested.

"I'll come with you," said Simolin.

"No, I will," I interjected, using my prerogative as superior. I wanted to get some fresh air. My brain was shutting down.

We were in luck. The car was parked out in front of the building. We took the elevator up to the fifth floor. There were several dents in the lower half of Mikkola's door, as if it had suffered from some kicking. Apparently someone on the outside had wanted to get in. I listened for a second, and then rang the doorbell. Nothing happened, and I pressed it a couple more times. It took half a minute before the door opened, and I could see Mikkola's hungover face in the crack. He smelt the cop on us and the look on his face grew even queasier.

"Criminal police," I said, confirming his fears. "The green Mondeo parked in front of the building is yours, isn't it?"

He gulped, exhaled a breath that reeked of stale booze, and said: "So?"

"You paid a visit to your former place of employment in that car yesterday morning."

His face blazed with guilt. This was no hardened criminal. "Fucking fuck. OK, I admit it, it was me, but that Jew deserved it. It was a witch hunt."

"You mind if we come inside?" I didn't wait for an answer; I just pushed my way in.

The place looked the way you'd expect for guy on a drinking binge. Fetid, funky air; stacks of newspapers, bottles and dishes. Waking up in surroundings like that doubled the agony of a hangover.

"Are you saying that Samuel Jacobson had it out for you?"

"Sami? No, Sami was a good guy; he understood that life isn't always peaches and cream. When he heard my old lady had split and taken my daughter with her, he came and talked to me. I'm talking about his scumbag son Roni. What an asshole. The drinking was obviously just an excuse. He wanted to get rid of me, and made up the drinking because there wasn't anything else."

"So you admit to placing the threatening letter in the company's mail box?"

"I guess there's no denying it. I got the idea when I read about those racists who'd been sending letters to Jews. OK, so it was stupid, but I'm a fair guy. You treat me right, I'll treat you right... Besides, I was pretty drunk... How did you find me?"

"It's what detectives do."

"Is it true that someone killed Sami? I've been drinking for four days straight. I've been blacking out, kind of going in and out of consciousness... Except when I took the letter. I was stone sober then," Mikkola added, once he realized what he had said.

"Yes, it's true," Stenman said. "We asked all of the employees at the company if they knew anything about it, for instance if they knew about any enemies Jacobson had, or threats he had received. So I'll go ahead and ask you, too, since we're here."

"The only thing I know about is this thing of mine. Believe me. It's already been a month since I was fired."

"You said Jacobson's son Roni had it in for you. Why?"

"Probably because I knew he was plotting against the old man. I heard him talking on the phone one day when he thought no one else was in the warehouse. He noticed me when I was leaving. Right after that he started spying on me, and when I took a little hair of the dog in the warehouse one day, he made a huge deal about it. I gave that company the best fifteen years of my life, and I get fired for one sip. Is that fair?"

"What did Roni say about his father over the phone?"

"Something like he had a way of getting rid of his dad… and that it wouldn't take long."

"Try to remember the details," I said. "Every word could be important."

Mikkola nudged a heap of clothes aside and lowered himself into a recliner. The effort winded him.

"He said… 'Dad's not going to be a problem much longer… someone promised to take care of it…'"

"Someone? Did he mention a name?"

"Might have, but I don't remember."

Mikkola's pained expression indicated that we wouldn't be squeezing anything else out of him. His gaze wandered over to a half-empty bottle of cheap cognac standing on the table.

I asked him to call if he remembered anything else. We had barely made it into the hallway before I heard the cascade of booze burbling down Mikkola's throat.

9

Because there were no investigative obstacles to burying Samuel Jacobson after the autopsy, I let the *chevra kadisha*, the congregation's burial society, claim the body.

I participated in the funeral in a dual role: as a Jewish acquaintance of Jacobson's and as a police officer.

Jacobson was a pillar of the community and had lots of friends. So there were lots of guests, too, about forty in all. I recognized most of them. A few non-Jews were also present, including Pekka Hulkko and a couple of Jacobson's business acquaintances.

Jewish funerals are austere affairs compared to Lutheran ones. Usually no one brings flowers, and Jacobson's coffin was made of the traditional unfinished pine without any fancy fittings or pillows. An uncomfortable last ride, but so far no one had come back to complain. Jacobson was swathed in a linen shroud and he was wearing a *tallit*, a prayer shawl. His head lay on soil from the Holy Land. I didn't know who'd had it ferried over from Israel, or how – in their luggage, or as cargo.

The point of the austerity was to serve as a reminder that death treated all men equally; none were rich or poor, none were obscure or famous – which of course wasn't true. Inequality existed, even in death.

Instead of flowers, every guest brought a stone to the graveside. I had picked mine from the shore the evening before. It was oval and polished by the sea, and felt good in my palm.

Even the Jewish cemetery looked somehow untended compared to Lutheran cemeteries. This was not a sign of indifference, however; just the opposite. Remembering the deceased plays an important role in Judaism, but life after death doesn't receive as much attention as in the neighbouring religion. No one was waiting to be admitted to heaven; there was also no fear of hell. Still, most Jews believed that an accounting awaited all men after death, where one's good and bad deeds would be justly weighed. You'd be rewarded for the good ones; for the bad, you'd pay dearly.

Before Jacobson's coffin could reach its final resting place, we recited psalms in the chapel and a eulogy was given. After the coffin had been lowered into the ground, I took my turn tossing three shovelfuls of dirt onto it. The faint thud of the sand hitting the lid was one of the most final sounds in this world. It was akin to the sound of a lock being primed before the executioner's shot, and the noise the removal of the pin made right before the grenade exploded.

After the grave had been filled and the temporary wooden plaque was in place, the rabbi read the traditional psalms. Then Roni, as a male relative, recited the Kaddish.

In other words, Jacobson's funeral didn't diverge from the usual formula, so I concentrated on the funeral guests, most of whom I knew. My brother Eli and his family were among the crowd, as were Max and his family. Jacobson's daughter Lea was there with her children. Evidently her husband hadn't made peace with his father-in-law, because he had stayed behind in Israel. Roni was there with his new wife and young daughter.

Once the other guests had left, I went and visited the graves of my father, my mother and my sister Hannah. I had been much closer to Hannah – who had been three years my junior – than to Eli, and so her suicide had been rough on me. I still missed her. I believed that if Hannah had been allowed to live, she would have accomplished much. She was by far the most gifted of the three descendants of Wolf Kafka.

After the funeral, coffee was served at a restaurant in Etu-Töölö. The moment I had my cup in my hand, Eli sidled up to me.

"What a boring funeral," he said. "Whatever happened to the renowned Jewish sense of humour?"

"So who's stopping you? Why don't you entertain us?"

Eli was right, though. I had attended funerals that were more fun.

Silberstein, the congregation chair, almost walked past us, but then he stopped to shake Eli's hand. He satisfied himself with nodding at me, even though he immediately took advantage of the situation and started asking about the Jacobson investigation.

"Nothing conclusive has come up yet," I said.

"It's hard to believe that it could be just a normal murder," Silberstein mused.

I noted that there was no such thing as a normal murder.

"I was referring to Jacobson's Jewishness. He was a man of influence in the congregation."

"We haven't discovered anything that would lead us to believe that Jacobson's Jewishness was in any way related to the crime."

I was starting to get annoyed that all my acquaintances felt the need to make Jewishness the motive for the murder.

"I find that rather surprising," Silberstein said grudgingly.

"What do you mean?" I asked, just to egg him on.

"I've known Samuel for such a long time... I can't think of any other reason. He was a good man, a good Jew, a good member of the congregation, a good father and husband... Who could have had any reason to kill him?"

My reaction was that not even Jacobson could be as much of a saint as Silberstein was making him out to be. "There are so many things about people we don't know," I said, even though I knew this would irritate Silberstein even more.

"I believe I knew Samuel," he said. There was an unmistakable edge in his voice.

Eli gazed past us, uncomfortable. I could tell he wished he were somewhere else.

"I'll see you tomorrow," Silberstein said to Eli, stalking off. It was then that I realized that antagonizing Silberstein had been stupid. I'd have to talk to him about Jacobson's role in the congregation, and he wasn't the type to forget easily.

"Like I said, it was a pretty boring funeral, so I think I'll head out, too." Eli went to get his overcoat, and left.

I had noticed Max eyeing me tentatively. When my gaze circled back around to him, he made up his mind and walked over, coffee cup in hand.

"Did Eli leave?" he asked, just to say something.

"Yup."

The follow-up question was easy to guess. "How are things going with the Jacobson case?"

"We found the getaway vehicle, but the motive is still unclear. As a matter of fact, I was going to drop by for a chat —"

"Or an interrogation?" Max finished. He tried to smile, but the muscles in his cheek started to twitch.

I had always found Max slightly comical, and this instance was no exception.

"As a matter of fact, to talk to you about Jacobson's loan. You brokered it."

"Eli told you?"

"No, Jacobson's wife, son and chief financial officer did. Is that enough? Why was he going to pay off the loan and take out one from a Finnish bank instead?"

"He was?"

"Yes. His wife told me."

"Maybe he thought that Estonian companies aren't reliable enough during a recession. He asked me about it once. That's the extent of what I know."

"What sort of company is Baltic Invest?"

Max vacillated a moment before answering: "Decent enough."

"Even though it's being investigated in Israel?"

Max was clearly unwilling to discuss the matter, but not responding would have seemed suspicious.

"That's all just internal politics. The Labour Party is trying to get people to believe it's the only honest party in the government.

Amos Jakov and Benjamin Hararin have been turned into scapegoats."

"According to the *Jerusalem Post*, Hararin is Jakov's stooge, and Jakov's companies are laundering Russian mafia money. Baltic Invest was also mentioned."

"No evidence was found. I heard that the investigation had been closed."

"The paper claimed that Jakov bribed and used his political contacts to pressure the police into ending the investigation."

"There's no evidence of anything of the sort."

I told him that we had found the car the killer had used and figured out who the owner was: Baltic Invest.

The news didn't fluster Max in the least.

I continued. "It's been reported stolen. Strange coincidence, wouldn't you say? I'd like to meet later to talk a little more about Jacobson's loans and some other matters."

"What other matters?"

"I'll explain then."

"I don't have anything to hide."

In my experience, men who said they had nothing to hide were the very ones who did.

"Ari!" I heard a familiar voice, and turned around. Lea walked up and, to my surprise, hugged me.

She looked weepy and twenty years older. I just looked twenty years older. She pulled back as soon as she felt how stiffly I reacted to her embrace.

"Do you remember Max?" I asked her.

"Of course."

Max backed away. "I have to go – client meeting."

"I'll call you later."

"When? I'm pretty busy today…"

"Early evening."

Max nodded at Lea, and exited without another word.

Lea and I looked at each other. Her jawline had softened, and there were wrinkles under her eyes. Her brown eyes were still amazingly bright and girlish, just like I remembered. I could sense an awkwardness between us, at least on my part. I also felt like my balding crown was as conspicuous as a zit on the side of a teenager's nose, and that my love handles were bulging out from under my shirt.

"Don't look at me so closely. I've grown old and wrinkled," Lea said shyly.

"You've matured."

"In other words, put on weight."

"Your first loves never grow old…"

A smile flickered across Lea's face, then vanished. "Mom said that you're investigating Dad's case. Have you discovered anything? I heard about the threats Dad received."

I told her what I had told Roni: that we didn't believe that anti-Semitism was the motive for the murder. I didn't even want to mention Mikkola to Lea.

"What's the motive, then?" Lea wondered.

"We don't know yet. I have to ask you a few questions about your father's company," I said. "You've been in regular contact, I understand."

"I know you'll have to talk to me, too. When?"

"As soon as possible."

"How about this evening? Does that work?"

"That's perfect. It was nice to see you. I want to hear more about your life when we talk later."

"Same here."

We agreed on a place and time. I paid my respects to Ethel, and made my exit. I had left work in the middle of the day to attend.

When I walked out onto the street, I saw Eli and Max standing next to Eli's car, engaged in a heated conversation. It almost looked like they were arguing.

I would have loved to have heard what they were talking about.

10

"The telecommunications data came in," Simolin said, waving a stack of paper. He was as eager and energetic as ever. Simolin was the sort who would still be that way when he was eighty years old and in the nursing home. It was in the genes.

"Have you had time to look it over?"

"It just got here half an hour ago."

"So in other words, you have."

"The mast data indicates pre-paid calls spread evenly across central Helsinki, which means that the locations of the calls were selected intentionally to prevent any clusters from forming. Jacobson received the final call the morning he was shot. It only lasted thirty seconds. There were a total of five calls over three days."

"Which parts of central Helsinki?"

"One from Töölö, one probably from Punavuori, one from Hakaniemi. It's impossible to say for sure about the other two; they could have come through different base stations."

"None from Estonia?"

"Nope, at least not in the data we have so far. That same day, Jacobson made two calls to the office, one to his wife, three to the Jewish congregation, one to attorney-at-law Max Oxbaum and one to Tel Aviv, Israel. I haven't had time to figure out all the calls yet. At least thirty were made over a two-to-three-day period, and I have a month's worth of call data."

"Has anything else caught your eye?"

"Roni Jacobson called his father from Lapland twice the day before he died, and his father called back twice…"

My cell phone rang. It was Jacobson's grey-haired neighbour, the one who loitered at his window and had seen the killer. "I heard something. It might be a rumour, but I thought I'd call just in case... you never know..."

I imagined the guy talking into the phone from his perch at the window, hawk-eyeing passers-by.

"I'd love to hear it."

"Those boys who found the car. I heard that they saw the killer. One of the boys lives nearby, and his sister walks our dog Titi. She said that her brother had seen the killer but their mother told him not to tell the police so the boy wouldn't get mixed up in anything. I wouldn't put a whole lot of stock in the boy, now, but Maija's a good girl. She wouldn't lie to me."

"Which boy are we talking about?"

"The Wallius boy. Jari."

I knew that the boys had been questioned and they had claimed that they hadn't seen anyone.

I thanked the man, and asked him to keep his eyes open. The case wasn't over yet.

I suspected my request would lead to him setting up a sentry station at the kitchen window and making a note of everyone who moved in the vicinity. Why not? It couldn't hurt, that was for sure.

I grabbed Simolin and we headed out to eastern Helsinki.

The Wallius residence was on the same side of the street as the Jacobsons', but a little closer to the heart of Tammisalo. It was only a few years old: white brick and lots of glass. Latter-day Aalto replica. The woman who answered eyed us suspiciously through the barely open door. I pulled out my badge and introduced us.

"Yes. What is it?"

"Your son found the car we were looking for. I'd like to talk to him about it."

"He already told everything to the police."

"But not to the investigators. I'm the lead investigator, and this is my colleague," I said, nodding at Simolin.

"Do you have a warrant?" the woman asked, still barricaded behind the door.

"A warrant for what?"

"A warrant to interrogate a minor. My husband is a lawyer —"

"We're not interrogating anyone. At this point, he's just an eyewitness."

A case about twenty years old crossed my mind, in which a thirteen-year-old boy had been found stabbed to death in a fort behind his house. I had gone around to all of the dead kid's friends', and the mother of one of the boys had done everything in her power to keep me from seeing her son. At first she told me he was sleeping, then she said he couldn't talk because he was in such severe shock. Eventually, I had been forced to resort to extreme measures. Within fifteen minutes, I knew that the boy had killed his friend. I could tell that the mother knew it too; she had tried to protect her child to the last.

In the end, Mrs Wallius grudgingly let us in and called for her boy. He didn't look the least bit afraid; on the contrary, he was excited. According to the neighbour, the boy was about eleven years old.

"Can we talk in your room?"

We followed the boy, the mother at our heels. I stopped and told her that we'd like to talk to the boy alone.

"Why? What are you trying to do?"

"Solve a murder. If you don't have any objections, that is…"

The mother was forced to back down.

The boy took a seat on his bed; Simolin and I pulled up wheeled office chairs from the desk. A war game was exploding on the computer screen. Simolin glanced at it.

"I have that. Pretty good, huh?"

"Which version, One or Two?"

"One."

"Two's even better, and harder."

I interrupted their conversation. "Could you tell me once more where you found the car?"

"From the start?"

"From the start. Every single detail. I think you've got a pretty good memory."

"I do."

"Are you the one who saw the car first?" Simolin asked.

"Yeah. Sami was pretty far behind me... We went there to eat plums. Otherwise they get rotten because nobody picks them..."

"I like plums, too," I said.

"They're really good: sweet and juicy," the boy said. "I was the first one in the Seppäläs' yard; we came through the back, by the hedge —"

"Wait a minute."

I pulled a notebook from my pocket and sketched from memory: the house, the garage, and their locations on the plot.

"Use this to show me where you came from."

The boy drew a line that followed the west side of the house and circled around to the front.

"This is where the plum tree is," he said, drawing a circle on the paper. "I was picking some plums from the ground, and when I stood up I saw that the garage door was ajar. I could see the trunk of a blue car with a Volkswagen symbol. Sami's kind of a wuss, so he didn't catch up to me till then."

"So then what did you two do?"

"We ate some plums and went home."

"That early?"

"I had to study for a test."

"Did you get a closer look at the car?"

"No. Sami got scared and said that he was going to leave, no matter what. So I went with him."

"Has there ever been a car in the garage before when you've gone to eat plums?"

"Never. No one's lived there for a long time, at least three years."

"And what about when you came home?"

"My sister came home from school and said that someone had killed Mr Jacobson and that the cops… the police were looking for a blue Golf. I told Mom that there was a blue Volkswagen in the Seppäläs' garage, the same kind the police were looking for. She called the police, and they came and got the car."

I eyed the boy thoughtfully. "So the garage door was ajar?"

"Yeah."

"When the police arrived, the door was closed. How is that possible? Did you close the door?"

"No, we scrammed."

"So who shut it, then?"

"I don't know."

"Probably the same guy who you and your friend saw."

"We didn't see any guy… We —"

"Sami said you saw a man in the yard."

"What? We said we wouldn't tell the —"

"That you wouldn't tell the police, huh?"

"Yeah. Mom said the guy's a killer and he might come after us. Sami almost started bawling."

Jari Wallius was clearly made of tougher stuff than his friend. He didn't appear bothered by the fact that he had been caught lying to the police.

"That was wrong. You can get punished for lying to the police."

The kid smiled, as if to show he knew we weren't serious. "Like what, prison?"

"Not that bad, but you're not going to get any points for lying, either. Now tell me what you saw."

The boy thought for a moment, brow furrowed, and then said: "Everything went like how I said at first, but when I got to the plum tree I saw the guy. He was just closing the garage door. Then he went behind the house and left that way."

"In another car?" Simolin asked.

"He was walking."

"Walking?"

"Yeah. He looked a little suspicious, so I went and looked in the garage and saw the car."

"Tell me more about the guy. How old was he, how was he dressed?"

"At least as old as you, maybe even older, normal height, pretty thin. He was wearing blue sweatpants and a blue Nike baseball cap."

"What brand were his sweatpants?" Simolin asked.

"Adidas, I think."

"Was he carrying a backpack or a bag or anything?"

"Yeah, a black backpack."

"Do you remember what brand?"

"There wasn't one, or else the logo was so small I didn't see it."

"Do you remember anything else? Hair, beard, moustache, glasses?"

"Short hair, dark, I think. He didn't have a moustache or a beard, but he had sideburns to at least halfway down his ear. He had sunglasses on. The kind cyclists wear."

"Could you draw the glasses?" I asked.

The boy did as asked. The picture turned out well.

"You know how to draw," I said, putting the sketch in my pocket.

"Yeah, I like drawing."

"So the man left on foot down the other side of the hill, towards the church?" Simolin asked.

"Yeah."

"Did you see where he turned?"

"No, I just made sure he left, and then Sami and me went to check out the car."

An idea occurred to me. "Could you draw a picture of the man? Draw everything you remember: the clothes, the backpack, everything. If you do a good job, we might be able to use it to identify him."

"Will I get a reward if you find him?"

"Maybe."

The kid was bursting with enthusiasm as he picked up the pen. It glided nimbly across the paper, and an image began to take shape. I was a horrible draughtsman myself, and had no idea how someone could create a recognizable portrait with just a few strokes.

"You want me to colour the clothes?"

"Go for it."

The boy bent over the paper, a look of concentration on his face. It only took about five minutes, and the picture was ready. I looked at it, and had to admit it was good. Even the posture of the body was completely natural. The eyes were hidden behind sunglasses, but the chin was narrow and long, and the nose slightly hooked.

"You could be an artist when you grow up. Did the guy have a bump in his nose?"

"Yeah. I saw it when he turned sideways. He was skinny, the way athletes are. I think he works out a lot and is in pretty good shape."

I thanked the boy. The mother was sitting on the sofa, but bounded up as soon as we came out of the bedroom.

"You should have told us that your son saw the man who left the car," I said in a reprimanding tone.

The woman's face turned beet red. "I was afraid the murderer might do something if he heard —"

"You've seriously compromised our investigation. Thanks to you, the killer has had a significant head start."

The woman's eyes widened. "I'm so sorry —"

"We're going to visit your son's friend Sami now. I'm going to ask you to make sure that your son doesn't call him. If he does, we'll be forced to take unpleasant measures —"

The woman rushed to assure us: "I won't let him call. I'm so sorry."

We went and visited Sami, but he couldn't give us any fresh

information. I showed him the drawing and he said he thought the man in the drawing looked exactly right.

When we were back at HQ, I made a few colour copies of the drawing and asked Simolin to scan it and put it online for all the patrols.

I was trying to figure out how to use the pictures most effectively when Huovinen stepped into my office. I showed him the drawing, and told him where I had got it.

"This is good. The kid can draw."

"I was wondering if I should release the sketch to the papers, or if it would be better to hunt the guy on our own."

Huovinen took another look at the picture. "Let's wait until 7 p.m., and if we haven't found anything by then, send it out. That'll be enough time for it to make it into the evening news and tomorrow's papers. The most important thing is getting any information we can on the guy. How'd the funeral go?"

"Most people consider Jacobson's murder an act of anti-Semitism."

"Pretty understandable."

"I'm meeting Jacobson's daughter at seven."

"Your former girlfriend, you mean," Huovinen said, a twinkle in his eye. Either Simolin or Stenman had spilled the beans. "How has she held up?"

"Pretty well."

"Then watch your step."

11

A water bus full of tourists was gliding under the Degerö bridge. The canal was so narrow that only a couple of feet remained on either side of the vessel, and the waves it created sloshed up the stone banks. A little further off, two boats were waiting to enter the canal. The tourists waved at Lea and me good-naturedly. We were standing side by side on the bridge, leaning against the railing. I got momentarily lost in nostalgia, and was on the verge of lowering my hand to her shoulder like I used to. Luckily I realized what was happening, and stopped myself in time. Huovinen's words came back to me: *Watch your step.*

"It looks exactly the same. It smells the same, too," Lea said. A gust of wind tousled her dark hair. For a brief instant, distant memory clouded the present moment and she was the young girl whom I had dated over twenty years ago.

"Maybe this spot looks the same, but nothing else does. Everything has changed. Helsinki has totally changed; I've changed – even though I'm actually a young man in a middle-aged man's body."

Lea glanced at me. "It's for the best. Middle age suits you."

"How about you?"

"A lot of things happen over twenty years. Too many."

"True. You like living in Israel?"

"Most of the time."

"Do you visit Finland often?"

"Once or twice a year. The next time I was supposed to come was for Dad's birthday in November… It's hard to believe that he's not here any more. He's always been there… my whole life."

We strolled slowly towards Laajasalo.

"The motive," I said. "We don't have a motive yet. If we knew the motive, I think we'd be able to make pretty rapid progress. It's hard to understand why someone would want to kill your father…"

"It's even harder for me than it is for you. Unless it's an act of anti-Semitic violence, which you say you don't think it is. Maybe I don't even want to try and think of an explanation, since it's my father."

"I get that, but I hope you'll try anyway…"

"You can be sure I've already discussed it with both Mom and Roni. None of us can come up with a believable reason for the crime. Nothing but guesses. Mom even imagined that Dad had another woman. Dad, another woman… Mom has always been jealous of Dad…"

"Your father was afraid of something, and who would he talk about it with if not his loved ones?"

"Not me, at least. Maybe Mom misunderstood and thought Dad was afraid of something, even though something else was going on. Dad was a good man; he didn't have any enemies."

He had one, at least, I thought.

"Your mother said that your father had warned her against opening the door to strangers. It's not likely that your mother misunderstood that. Besides, the fear was rational. The killer was dressed as a police officer. There can be no other explanation except that that's how he got your father to open the door. Your father was on his guard because he was afraid."

"I suppose I'll have to take your word for it."

"Your brother left for Lapland a day before your dad started staying home from the office. Could that have something to do with all this?"

"What on earth are you implying?" Lea asked, although I knew she understood perfectly well what I was implying.

"Maybe he also believed Roni was in danger, and sent him away."

"Roni wouldn't have lied to me… or to Mom."

"Maybe Roni didn't know what was going on. Maybe your dad had just asked or demanded that he take his vacation right when he did."

"If that were the case, Dad would have told Roni the real reason. It'd be easier for him to avoid danger if he were anticipating it. And if that were the case, why wasn't Dad scared for Mom?"

"Perhaps because your brother and father were caught up in the same imbroglio, but your mother wasn't."

"You don't respect Roni very much, do you? Since you think he would hold something back that would help you catch Dad's murderer."

"Why didn't your father contact the police if he was afraid, then?"

"I don't know. You tell me," Lea said.

"Because he would have been forced to explain something to the police that he wanted to keep under wraps. And that something was to do with him or your brother, or both. Maybe he ended up footing the bill for your brother… Maybe he was killed as a warning to your brother. Regardless of what my opinion is of Roni, it's easier for me to believe that the murder has something to do with him than with anything your father did or did not do."

My words gave Lea pause. And that had been the point. I was trying to get her to see things more clearly.

Two little boys were digging for worms in the woods. The alders lining the shore were still green, but the nip of early autumn was unmistakable. The last couple of nights had been cold. There had already been night frosts in Lapland, and it had snowed in the fells.

Eventually Lea spoke. "That was a cruel thing to say; Roni is my brother."

"And I'm a police officer. Sometimes we have to say cruel things. A little over a year ago your brother built a big, expensive house in Marjaniemi. Do you know where he got the money?"

"He sold his old home and took out a loan. Dad thought the house Roni was building was too expensive and the loan he took out was too big. I presume Roni makes a pretty good living. He is an executive, after all."

"When was the last time you were in touch with your father?"

"A week… five days ago. Dad called in the evening. We talked for about ten minutes."

"What about?"

"Completely ordinary things. Were things calm in Tel Aviv, how the kids were doing, were they enjoying school, how I was doing. Then he told me was in good health and Mom was, too. Roni and his new wife were not doing very well, evidently. He always told me whom he had seen at synagogue… He even mentioned you…"

"Me?"

"Yes. He said that there had been an article about you in the paper. You had solved a taxi murder."

"That was over two months ago."

"He'd hear about you at the synagogue, from your brother. They were on some committee together."

"The executive council?"

"Evidently. That's why they saw each other a lot."

"Eli has always had a big mouth. Did your dad say how the company was doing?"

"He mentioned that there was a recession in Finland and things weren't looking too good. But he had made it through the last recession and he intended to make it through this one, too…"

"Which reminds me. How did Roni react when your dad wanted to stay on as CEO?"

"Roni, Roni, Roni. I don't know; we haven't talked about it. It would have only been a year or two at most."

"Your father didn't seem concerned about anything?"

"Not to me. When we ended the call, he said to say hello to everyone and reminded me that we'd see each other for his birthday."

"We found the car that the killer used. It turned up right near your folks' house."

"Roni told me about that. A pretty unusual place... Audacious."

"The car was stolen. From Estonia."

"Is the killer Estonian?"

"We don't know. It's possible. The car is owned by an investment firm based in Estonia, the same company that financed the construction of the new building for your dad's company."

Lea stopped and stared at me with her chocolate-brown eyes. It reminded me how beautiful they seemed to me when I was young... and still seemed to me now. "So what? You don't believe it's a coincidence?" she asked.

"It could be, but it's a pretty strange coincidence. The company is owned by an Israeli businessman named Benjamin Hararin. You've probably heard of him..." Now it was my turn to stare at Lea.

"I have. Every Israeli has."

"But Hararin is considered a straw man. The real owner of the company is the Israeli billionaire Amos Jakov. I suppose you've heard of him, too. He's suspected of having contacts in the Russian mafia. It's easier to list what he doesn't own than to list what he does."

Lea's face went rigid. "Are you trying to offend me? If you are, you've succeeded," she said, a cold gleam in her eye.

"What do you mean? I don't understand..." I stammered, genuinely mystified.

"Are you trying to tell me you're not aware that my husband is a director at the finance company owned by Jakov? Your brother and Max Oxbaum can thank him that they acquired representation rights in Finland. That's why Dad took the loan through them. Roni, too."

"I had no idea. Eli didn't say a word. I didn't even know that your brother had taken out his loan through them."

Lea's tone was barbed. "He did. It's been almost two years now. My husband arranged him a loan with favourable terms. That might explain why he was able to manage it."

I considered what Lea had just revealed to me. I had been telling the truth when I told her I had no idea that her husband was a director at Baltic Invest. All I knew was that he worked for Hararin. If Jacobson had basically got the loan from his son-in-law and for a good price, why would he have wanted to switch to a different one? Had his son-in-law warned him about the investigation by the Israeli police after all? Or had Jacobson heard unfavourable things about Baltic Invest via some other route and made the call to pull up stakes himself? I decided to get straight to the point.

"If the loan your husband arranged is so inexpensive, why would your father want to take out a new loan from a Finnish bank and get out of the old one?"

"Who said so?" Lea asked, vertical lines running between her dark brows.

"He had mentioned it to both your mother and his CFO, Pekka Hulkko. Roni was aware of it as well."

"I hadn't heard… Dad never talked to me about things like that. Are you sure?"

I nodded. I didn't dare to tell her about her father's email message to Roni at this point. It didn't leave any room for doubt. "Can you guess what the reason might be?"

"I can certainly ask my husband if —"

"Don't bother, at least for the meantime. Were your father and your husband on good terms?"

"I think so. They'd butt heads now and again and disagree about some things…"

I had made Lea worried. I could see it in her every gesture.

"Could your husband have mentioned something to your father that would have scared him… warned him about something, for instance?"

100

"You talk as if my husband were a gangster. I don't know about anything like that... I'd better get back to Mom..."

My phone rang. I glanced at the screen and didn't recognize the number. I went ahead and answered anyway. It was Max.

"Hi. Can I call you back later?"

"You said you wanted to see me. I'm free now..."

"Where are you?"

"At the office. But we could meet at my boat. It's at the Lauttasaari marina."

Max sounded like he really wanted to meet me. Just a few hours earlier it had been just the opposite. His tone was almost pleading. "I'd like to talk in confidence. I might be able to help you with your investigation, but unofficially. No one can ever find out, and I'll never agree to testify... And you're coming alone, right?"

"Fine. Is 8:30 all right?"

"I'll be waiting on my boat. It's at the C Dock. I'll leave the door open. Slip forty-five."

"See you there," I said, and hung up.

I escorted Lea to her gate. She stopped and stood there eyeing me coolly, with her arms crossed.

"If you have any evidence against my husband, I'd like to hear about it."

"Let's talk again later. Say hello to your mother."

I watched Lea walk away. I had forced her to think about things from a new perspective, but I wasn't sure whether it would help or hinder the investigation.

12

What could Max want to tell me? I wondered the whole brief trip from one edge of town to the other. Max was one of the last people I could imagine revealing sensitive information about himself. He was an indulgent hedonist who denied himself nothing, annoyingly self-aware and completely blind to his own faults. As far as I could tell, Max's bar for guilt was set extremely high.

He owned a thirty-foot fibreglass yacht, and had for years. However, he preferred spending time at the yacht club's restaurant hobnobbing with its elite members to being at sea. This was also apparent on his boat, which looked like it had been decorated for society functions. I knew, because I had been invited to Max's parties a couple of times.

Like the other big boats, the boat was moored crosswise at the end of the dock. The marina had security, but there was no one in sight. The area was so large that the guard hut was almost a hundred yards away.

The steel-mesh door to C Dock was open, so I didn't need to call Max to come and open it.

I marched down the rocking pier, checking out the boats. Eli wasn't the only one who dreamt of buying one. I'd thought about it myself. I wanted a speedy little number that would take me out to an island in minutes to drop a line. Not to fish; to angle with a hook and worm. That was enough for me. I didn't live far from the marina, and could conceivably get a slip within walking distance.

You couldn't help but notice Max's boat; it was hands-down the handsomest on the dock. It must have cost a couple of hundred thousand euros. It was Norwegian-made and had all the amenities to make life on board comfortable, including an ice machine and a well-stocked bar whose mahogany walls were lined with humorous brass placards, like *Bar Open: Midnight – 11 p.m.*

It was getting dark, and I could see there was a light on in the cabin. A school of small fish sent the surface of the water skittering; the sea smelt heavy but intoxicating. Once when I was at the marina with Dad when I was little, he told me that if I listened very closely, the sea would tell me its secrets. It would tell me of sunken ships, of golden treasure, of pirates and Indians living on the other side of the world, of kings and princesses. The stories had travelled with the waves for hundreds of years, and now they were here. Then he lifted his hand to his ear and asked me to listen too. He described everything so vividly that I really imagined I could hear the sea telling those stories to me.

The pontoons creaked and swayed under my feet. I breathed in the salt smell of the deeps. Maritime life had its appeal.

I saw movement out of the corner of my eye and turned. A figure dressed in dark clothes and a hoodie leapt from Max's boat to the dock and ran to its seaward end. He didn't look back.

"Hey! Stop —"

The figure stopped and turned. I saw him raise one of his hands. It took an instant before I understood what he was doing. I threw myself onto the dock stomach-first and the bullet whizzed over my head, striking the dock. The gun had a silencer; all I heard was the sound of the bullet's impact and its ricochet.

I had landed in an awkward position and it took agonizingly long to draw my weapon, so long that I could feel my guts wrench in panic. The guy had plenty of time to shoot again if he wanted to. But there was no second shot. By the time I twisted myself around in his direction, gun in hand, he had disappeared.

I kept scanning as I warily crept to the end of the dock, gun at the ready. I heard a splash and saw a blue kayak flash between some boats. The kayak slipped behind them and raced off in the direction of the West Harbour. By the time I caught sight of it again, it was almost a hundred yards away. For a second I considered going after the shooter, but I knew that in just a minute he would be on the opposite shore making his escape, whereas I would have to pursue him in my car, looping around several kilometres across the bridge.

I pulled out my phone and tapped in the emergency number. As I waited for a response, I walked back to Max's boat. I rapped on the bow rail and called out: "Max!"

No one answered. The waves slapped against the yacht's hull and the dock. Normally the sound would have been soothing, but not now.

"Max!" I called out again, climbing aboard. The heavy vessel barely moved under my weight.

I peered in through one of the cabin windows. I saw the lounge decorated in exotic woods and velvet.

Max was sitting on the sofa, bent forward. There was a whisky bottle on the table in front of him. I knocked on the window, but Max didn't move a muscle.

I circled around the lounge and climbed down to the rear deck. The teak door was ajar. I stepped in and felt soft, heavy carpeting under my feet.

"Max!"

Max still didn't move, but now the reason was obvious. There were two bullet holes in his left temple only a quarter of an inch apart. Just then, emergency response answered. It was the best timing ever in my entire career as police officer.

I requested several patrols to look for the killer who had fled by kayak, and warned them that he was dangerous. After that I called Simolin, even though I knew he had put in a long day. I also called Huovinen at home. We agreed that I would lead the investigation, because the incident was apparently linked to the Jacobson case. Huovinen promised to send rein-forcements.

After I had made the calls, I sat down on the sofa across from Max. I had sat on that very sofa before, but it had been in much more jovial company. One of Max's eyes was slightly open, and I could see the light reflecting off of it. His head was angled and his back was hunched, like a man already weighed down by sorrow and tribulation who was anticipating the final blow with complete indifference. At least death brings the gift of comforting oblivion.

It was only now that I realized that Max was, despite all his bravado and egotism, a knight of doleful countenance.

I stood up and went off in search of the security guard. I found him in his hut, flipping through a boating magazine and sipping coffee. Sandwiches waited on the table. The heater was on, and the hut was stiflingly hot.

The guard was a sixty-year-old man wearing a turtleneck sweater, a black baseball cap and short rubber boots. The night's forecast was for rain. I introduced myself and asked when he had last done a round. He looked flustered, and didn't know what to say.

"Did crazy old Heikkilä call you again? It's not worth calling in the police just because I'm a tiny bit late, is it? He said that life vests had been stolen from his boat and that I'm the one responsible…"

I reassured him that this was about something completely different, something much more serious. Evidently I chose the wrong words, because he didn't appear reassured.

"Why don't you just tell me when you last did a round?"

"Half an hour ago."

"Did you see anything out of the ordinary?"

"What should I have seen?"

"Did you go out on C Dock?"

"Of course."

"And you didn't see anything out of the ordinary?"

The guard was dismayed. "I don't understand what you're getting at."

I told him that a body had been found on a boat on C Dock.

The man's face went white, and he put his coffee cup down.

"It's not my fault. I was late because my wife didn't bring the car home on time. She was supposed to be home by 5:30 at the latest, but —"

His explanations carried a hint of panic.

I cut him off. "I'm not blaming you for anything. Tell me about this evening. What have you done since you arrived at the marina?"

The man tossed the boating magazine onto the table.

"The guard's supposed to go around to all of the docks and make sure that the boats are properly secured. I did my rounds half an hour ago and didn't notice anything out of the ordinary. Did you say C Dock? The lights were on in Oxbaum's boat, and he looked like he was in there. That's not a crime, so I let him be."

"What do you mean, looked like?"

"I saw someone moving around inside. The curtains were drawn, and I assumed it was Oxbaum."

"Did you see Oxbaum arrive at the marina?"

"It was around seven."

"And he was alone?"

"Yes."

"Did you see anyone else?"

"No... maybe someone came in while I was in the bathroom."

"Not even in a canoe?"

"I know I didn't see a single person in a canoe."

"How long were you in the bathroom?"

"About ten minutes. My stomach's been a little hard lately. I tried to get someone to cover for me, but no one could make it. It's not my fault if... The harbourmaster came by and said hello around 6:30, when he was taking a new gas cylinder out to his boat, but I guess he doesn't count. There were probably other folks here, too. This is a big marina and folks come down here in the evenings to fish, but I didn't pay any attention to them because nothing out of the ordinary happened…"

I wonder what it would have taken for the guard to have noticed anything.

"So what time did you see someone moving around on Oxbaum's boat?"

The guy glanced at his watch. "About 8 p.m. The round began at eight."

"What time did your shift start?"

"Six… but I was fifteen minutes late because my wife —"

"The gate to C Dock was open when I got here. Did you close it behind you?"

"Of course… or I mean, I normally would have closed it, but Oxbaum asked me to leave it open because he was expecting a guest. He promised to shut it behind him. It's not my fault if —"

"Did Oxbaum came by car?"

"Yes, in that black Benz SUV of his. Parked it in the lot."

I saw two patrol cars turn into the marina.

"I'll be right back. Stay here in the hut."

The man was clearly interested in seeing a real body. He looked disappointed. "I have to inform the harbourmaster about this."

"Tell him to come here. I want to talk to him. Don't talk to anyone else yet."

I went and explained the situation to the police. While we were talking, Simolin drove into the marina, followed by the forensic investigators. I led them to the yacht. Simolin stood on the dock, looking around.

"Expensive barge. You knew the owner?"

"He's my brother's business partner."

"And Jewish, based on the name."

"Yes."

"So he knew Jacobson, too, I guess?"

"Yes. This has to be related somehow," I said pensively.

"Small world," Simolin mused. "Pretty unusual. The killer flees by kayak. I haven't come across too many kayak killers in my day. On the other hand, it was a pretty ingenious move. Straight across the channel there and you're long gone, free and clear."

As soon as Simolin said *kayak killer*, I knew that's the exact phrasing the tabloids would use in their headlines.

"Did the bullet come close?" Simolin asked.

"Way too."

"What were you doing down here, anyway?"

I told him about Max's call.

"And he didn't hint as to what it was about?"

"No… He said he wanted to tell me something that would help me with the investigation. This morning at the funeral he was still claiming that everything was fine and he didn't know anything about anything."

"I wonder what made him change his mind?"

I didn't bother answering. I was mad at myself for not having raked Max over the coals and demanding more information on the phone.

The forensic specialist found footprints on the deck of the yacht. I told her that I had been inside and would definitely have left footprints on the deck, too. She took my prints for later comparison and elimination.

"Could you please check the pockets of the deceased? I need his car keys… and cell phone."

The investigator passed my request on to her colleague inside, and I got the keys.

"There's no phone. This victim was also shot with a .22, by the way. That means it could be the same perp as with the Tammisalo murder."

The matter would resolve itself as soon as tests were conducted on the bullet that would be retrieved from Max.

I thanked her and climbed back onto the dock. The first drops of rain fell softly on my face. It was almost dark now, and the city lights gleamed beyond the channel.

My phone rang. It was a patrol reporting that they had found the kayak potentially used by the killer at the West Harbour. There was no trace of the kayaker.

"I'll go have a look at the car before I leave," I said to Simolin. Oxbaum's car was in the lot, just like the guard had guessed. I circled it and looked in. Then I opened the door and climbed in behind the wheel. There was nothing on the seats, but there were a few CDs in the door compartment. I opened the glove box and emptied the contents onto the passenger seat. Meanwhile, Simolin examined the trunk.

Vehicle registration, a Swiss army knife, a parking fine in a plastic sleeve, a few parking stubs and a receipt from a gas station. It indicated that Max had bought thirteen litres of gas at the ABC service station in Vantaa. There was another receipt for two coffees from the same place. I shoved the receipts into the plastic sleeve containing the ticket, and put it in my pocket.

Simolin opened the door and looked in. "I found this in the spare tyre compartment," he said, showing me a small, battered handgun. "What would a lawyer need a gun for? Unless he was afraid of something… But why didn't he take it with him onto the boat?"

"Because he was expecting me." I took a closer look at the gun. I picked it up and examined it very carefully. Simolin handed me his LED lamp. The pistol was a 1938 Beretta. There was a chip in the right-side Bakelite plate, and the front of the grip had been roughened with a file.

The gun had been my father's. He had got it from his own father, who had brought it home from the war. It was one of thousands of illegal firearms that were souvenirs of the war.

I handed the weapon back to Simolin, who looked a little baffled at it.

We went back to the marina and I asked the forensic investigator to tow Max's car in for examination. I wanted them to get everything they could from it, down to the last fingerprint, hair, fibre and skin cell.

By now it was almost ten. I drove Simolin downtown so he could continue by bus to Puistola, where he and his girlfriend had just bought themselves a town house. He was excited about having his own sauna and about the hobby room that had been built in the basement. Someone at work had asked about a housewarming party, but Simolin had awkwardly dodged the question. He didn't want to admit such a large crowd of co-workers into his private sphere.

I was envious of the enthusiasm he had for so many things, which he could delve into at any time and escape the pressures of the job. I, on the other hand, had one final unpleasant task before me – or two, to be exact. First I had to inform Max's wife Ruth what had happened, and afterwards I had to pay Eli a visit. Then again, I guessed both meetings would be even more unpleasant for them than for me.

13

"Max murdered. I can't believe it," Eli said. He went so white I was afraid he would faint. He stared at me with a mixture of incredulity and fear. "I talked with him just a few hours ago," he said, hammering at his forehead as if trying to wake himself up from a dream.

We were at Eli's. He was alone; his wife was at the theatre and would be going out for dinner afterwards.

The living room was as big as a basketball court and had a view of the water. I was sitting on an expensive-looking leather armchair with a hardwood frame. I knew that the chair cost more than three months of my net salary.

"What did you talk about?"

"It had to be a hit," Eli insisted, not hearing my question. He was lost somewhere inside his head. "We've owned that company together for over fifteen years. Most people thought Max was annoying, but he wasn't actually as big an asshole as he seemed. I know you didn't like him."

Eli was right, but speaking ill of the dead wasn't the thing to do, so I kept my mouth shut.

"You said you talked just a few hours ago. I'd like to know what about."

"Have you already told Ruth?" Eli asked.

"Yes."

I was glad Eli didn't ask how Ruth had taken her husband's death, because she hadn't taken it at all well. Who would? She had sat there for a moment in silence, and then started wailing at the top of her lungs. It wasn't pleasant to watch or listen to.

I called her sister, who lived nearby, and stayed with Ruth until she showed up. The sister promised to call Max's children and have them come and be with their mother. Neither of them lived at home any more.

"What did you talk about?" I asked for the third time. Eli managed to shake himself out of his stupor.

"It was pretty strange, actually. Max called and asked if he could come by. He did, and he asked me to prepare the Jacobson loan papers, because Roni wanted to carry out his father's wishes: pay off the company's loan and take out a new one from a Finnish bank. I found that odd, because that had always been Max's job, and because he had assured me he had been able to get Roni to simmer down. Max said that he had to go out of town on business for a few days and wouldn't have time to take care of it."

"That was it?"

"What else should there be?"

"Dad's pistol."

"What about it?" Eli asked, avoiding my gaze.

"Did you give it to Max?"

"Yes. How did you know?"

"It was found in Max's car."

"That's just great," Eli snorted. "Are you going to tell whose weapon it is? It's not like it's on the books. I doubt anyone's interested in it; it's not the murder weapon, is it?"

"Luckily not. Both of us would be screwed if it were. Why the hell didn't you tell me about the gun?"

Eli was right in that the weapon was of no significance to the investigation proper. But the thought of concealing the gun's origins felt distasteful. I started fuming, at myself as well as Eli, and decided I'd tell Simolin and Huovinen about the weapon.

"There wasn't a good moment."

"There wasn't? It doesn't matter; I still have to tell my boss about it."

"Why? It won't look good if a well-known detective is found in possession of an illegal firearm," Eli said.

"Actually, the gun was in the possession of a well-known lawyer."

"It was both of theirs; a family heirloom."

"Why did Max need a gun?"

"He said he had received some threatening phone calls. Didn't give me any more details. I could tell he was really scared, so I gave him the gun. I shouldn't have, I know. But what's forcing you to be such a goody-two-shoes and tell about the pistol?"

Eli took a glass from the cocktail cart and poured in some expensive vintage whisky far beyond the reach of men like me. He offered me some too, but I declined.

"Goody-Two-Shoes," Eli repeated, taking a long swig.

"What time did you meet Max?"

"About six o'clock."

"Why then? Had he received another call?"

"Apparently."

That made sense, and would explain why Max had changed his mind and wanted to talk to me. He was afraid, and he figured that talking would be to his advantage. What I didn't understand was why he had asked Eli to prepare the loan papers for Jacobson's company. Maybe the papers were nothing more than a ruse to see Eli and ask for the gun.

"I saw you two on the street after the funeral. What were you discussing?"

"I asked Max if everything was all right. He seemed strange, subdued... I thought maybe he had taken something..." Eli realized he had said too much, and backpedalled. "He said he was just tired because he wasn't sleeping and was working too hard."

"We want more information on Jacobson's loan. You don't have a problem with that, I take it?"

"Who does? You do?" Eli stared at me coolly. "You're the one leading the investigation."

"Joint decision."

"You know full well I can't just give out that information. Corporate loans are confidential. Wouldn't it be easier to ask Roni?"

"Maybe I will. Have you ever met Benjamin Hararin, the owner of Baltic Invest?"

"Do we have to talk about this right now?"

"Yes. The more time passes, the harder it will be to solve the case."

"I don't get how this information is going to help you with that. OK, we met once. When Max and I were in Tel Aviv."

"By chance, or was it a business meeting?"

Eli had already emptied his glass, and poured himself more whisky. "This is starting to smell like an interrogation," he said morosely.

"It would be better for your sake if we talk now, not when it's too late."

"What do you mean, for my sake?"

"Leave the questioning to me. It's what I get paid for."

"Everything is off the record, then," Eli said petulantly. "It was a vacation, but when Hararin heard we were in town, he wanted to meet us."

"What was your impression of him?"

"Smart guy."

"What about Amos Jakov?"

"I haven't met him."

"But what do you think about him?"

"There's no smoke without fire. He's never denied the criminal contacts from his youth, but guys like that are a dime a dozen in Israel. That place has more mafiosi than Sicily."

"Do you believe Hararin takes orders from Jakov?"

"So it would seem. Seem, mind you, nothing more."

"Could Jacobson have borrowed money from Baltic Invest without your knowledge?"

"Maybe, but then it would've had to have happened somewhere besides Finland. Finland is our territory."

"But Baltic Invest doesn't use extreme collection methods?"

"We use the same collection agencies as everyone else, but I can definitely say that there were no payment problems with Jacobson that would have gone that far. Like I said, we came to an agreement about the late payments. That's why I don't understand why he wanted to switch to another lender."

"What else happened in Tel Aviv when you and Max were there?"

"What do you mean?"

"Did you do anything there you regret, you and Max?"

Eli looked at me, mouth hanging slightly. Suddenly his defences crumbled. He looked like someone who had been caught in a trap. It wasn't pleasant seeing my brother that way. Now I knew that my childhood friend Dan, who had worked for the Mossad, had told the truth about Eli and Max's escapades in Tel Aviv. Their sexual shenanigans had been videotaped, and someone had them in a headlock. The question was whether they had already been blackmailed.

"Actually there's no point in me asking, because I know you did. Have the videos already been used?"

"What videos?"

"The ones you don't want your wives to see. Have you and Max been blackmailed with them already?"

"Come on, leave it —"

"Maybe Max was being blackmailed into helping out with Jacobson's murder somehow, and when he refused, he was killed."

Eli didn't take my theory seriously. "Let's assume that Max screwed around and there was proof, say a video. So what? He's not going to help someone murder his friend just because he doesn't want his wife to watch the tape. I know what Ruth's like. Max knew how to twist her around his little finger."

"Maybe someone threatened to send the tapes to the leaders of the congregation?"

"That would have been a tougher spot for Max, but that's still no reason to become an accomplice to murder."

"Can you think of anything so major that it could have been used to blackmail Max?"

"No," Eli pouted.

"You told me that Max acquired the Baltic Invest representation through his connections. I heard from Lea that her husband arranged it because he wanted to help out his father-in-law."

"Max knew Lea's husband, Joel Kazan. It's almost the same thing."

"So it was Kazan who lured you into the honey trap?"

"Honey trap," Eli snorted. "He's the one who took us out in Tel Aviv, but I'm not sure about the after-party. There was so much going on, and so many people around. We were at Hararin's place at that point... there were a lot of people and a lot of women, really nice Jewish girls. Have you ever seen a blonde Jewish girl? There were a bunch of them there that night. They wanted to stay over... These things happen..."

"When did you find out that your antics had been secretly videotaped?"

Eli decided to reveal his hand. "About a month ago. Max found out – I don't know how – and told me. He promised to handle it one way or another. Of course I understood that the tapes were part of the picture, but he wouldn't tell me how. I thought everything was over, especially when Max said he had taken care of the problem. Evidently he hadn't."

"And you didn't ask how he had taken care of the problem?"

"Of course I did. He said that it was better if I didn't know. He wouldn't tell me. And I wanted to stay out of it, because no one had blackmailed me."

"Can you guess what it was about?"

"I think Max gave the killer some information that he used against Jacobson, and Max didn't realize until Jacobson's death that he had helped the murderer. It's dangerous to know who the murderer is, and it's even more dangerous to know who paid the murderer."

"Are you sure that you're not making the case and the motive too complicated? What if the murder was about money? What if Max embezzled funds from Baltic Invest and got caught? They didn't want to kill a golden goose – just Jacobson, who was causing problems anyway. As a warning."

Eli was clearly offended on behalf of his former partner. "You think you can treat me like some goddamn fungus: keep me in the dark and feed me shit? Max had enough money for the life he led. He had an inheritance, and it's not like Ruth comes from a poor family. Max didn't have any reason to embezzle anything from anyone."

"Maybe he had expensive hobbies: gambling, drugs, women?"

"He wasn't a saint, but I would have known if he had gambled and… a woman now and then wouldn't have sent him to the poorhouse."

I guessed the reason for Eli's evasion. "Did Max use drugs?"

"I had my suspicions. I think he used cocaine on occasion. Lots of people do in these circles."

It had been a long day, and I was getting tired. I was having a hard time keeping my thoughts collected.

"I think that's enough for tonight. We want the Jacobson loan papers, so if you'll set them aside…"

"Didn't Ruth have any ideas as to why…?"

"I couldn't ask her, not yet."

"Max's will is in the safe at the office, like mine. We agreed that the one who lived longer would handle the other's affairs."

"Does the will contain any surprises?"

"No, it's completely normal. Ruth and the kids get everything."

"For your sake, it would be best to let us know immediately if you remember anything that could help us. It might be something totally trivial. You haven't been very helpful up to this point."

I was pulling on my coat when Eli asked: "Are you buying a car?"

"No, why?"

"You didn't talk to Max about buying a car?"

"Nope. I haven't even seen him in months, except today at the funeral."

Eli stroked his jaw. "That's weird. I remembered something. When Max left, he asked me to say hello to you and tell you not to buy the same kind of Benz he has, because it guzzles thirteen litres per hundred kilometres, and you have to fill it up all the time."

14

The next day one more investigator joined the case when Detective Jari Oksanen returned from vacation. Oksanen was nuts about cars, and one of the driving forces behind the police rally club. He drove a customized Audi with an exhaust modification that must have been illegal, because the thundering and popping of the engine preceded his car by a hundred yards. I could hear it in my office when Oksanen turned onto Radiotie, accelerated the final yards, and plunged into the parking garage.

At the morning recap, I explained to Oksanen where we were with the case. He was as full of pep and energy as his over-tuned ride. All I had to do was channel that energy in the right direction. Oksanen required a little more steering than Stenman and Simolin, who carefully considered their every move. On the other hand, Oksanen's spontaneous blundering sometimes led to surprisingly good results. Either that, or he was exceptionally lucky.

We listened for a minute to Oksanen's most recent Formula One report, then forced the conversation back to work matters. I was just getting started when there was a knock at the door, and without waiting for a response, Huovinen stepped in.

"Got some interesting info."

Huovinen was smiling so broadly that whatever it was couldn't have been very serious.

"Takamäki's team solved the Seeds of Hate case. The kidnapped professor wrote the letters himself."

"Huh? Why?"

"He hit on one of his students at a party and went home with her. Her boyfriend walked in on them, clobbered the guy, and tossed him out in his underwear. The bloodied professor was looking for a cab when he ran into a patrol, and couldn't come up with anything except that he'd been kidnapped. He's married to a hot-blooded Spaniard, and didn't want to get busted for stepping out on her. To make the case seem more believable, he wrote a few racist threats the next day and sent them to relevant targets."

Oksanen guffawed.

"How did they figure that out?" Stenman asked.

"The boyfriend who kicked the professor's ass chucked the professor's stuff in a dumpster, where someone found it. Rocky's fingerprints were all over it. He'd had a previous assault conviction, so the police paid him a visit, and that was all she wrote."

"That professor's going to be sorry once the papers get hold of that story," Oksanen said, still chuckling.

I briefed Huovinen on the status of my case, and he went on his way.

Simolin had gone through all of Jacobson's telecommunications data; it hadn't revealed anything new. Max's phone hadn't been found, but the call data had already been requested. The examination of the killer's Golf had proved to be an investigative dead end, and the Estonian police didn't have anything new for us. The divers from Search and Rescue had hunted for the weapon on both sides of the bridge without any luck. The dives at the other bridge, the one that crossed the canal near the Tammisalo marina, were just beginning. The sketch that Jacobson's neighbour's kid had drawn of the killer had been shown on the ten o'clock news, and it was in both tabloids and the *Helsingin Sanomat* the next morning. Even though the picture was good, it hadn't generated a single solid tip.

Max's murder had also made the papers, despite the fact that we had agreed that it wouldn't be reported until tomorrow. From the information included in the articles, we deduced that the leak had been either the security guard or the harbourmaster. The tabloids were already talking about the second "Jewish killing" and wondering if the victims' Jewish background was just a coincidence. I drafted a brief release and sent it off to the STT, the national news agency.

In other words, the fourth day of the investigation had started off in somewhat depressing circumstances. Like you had blown a month's salary on lotto cards and ferociously scratched one after the other, only to have them all turn up blank.

"You think Oxbaum's murder is connected to the Jacobson killing?" Oksanen asked.

"One way or another," I said. "The National Bureau of Investigation promised results from the ballistics tests this afternoon. Then we'll know."

Oksanen had his own, completely new theory about events.

"What if Oxbaum shot Jacobson?" he enthused. "If Jacobson threatened to reveal something that would be bad for Oxbaum."

"Who killed Oxbaum, then?" Stenman asked. "Both were shot with a .22 calibre weapon, and Oxbaum had a 9 mm." Stenman found Oksanen's habit of thoughtlessly bandying about theories annoying.

"The description doesn't match Oxbaum; neither does anything else," I said. "I believe he felt guilty about Jacobson's death and thought that he had put other people's lives at risk. That's why he wanted to meet me. But the killer got there first."

"And just in the nick of time," Stenman said.

"That's quite the conspiracy theory," Oksanen said. "Did anyone besides you see this canoe guy?"

"The kayak was stolen from the marina, and it turned up at the West Harbour. Presumably the killer had a car there that he used to continue his journey. Unfortunately not a single eyewitness has turned up. No fingerprints were found on the kayak, or anything else that would help the investigation."

"Of course not." Oksanen sounded resentful, as if he thought it was unfair that the criminal hadn't left any clues behind. And maybe that is what he thought; who knew?

"You and Jari start by paying a visit to Oxbaum's secretary. Go through Max's office and bring in the computer and anything else necessary so we can check it out," I said to Simolin. "Arja and I will go see his wife. Simolin, you can also put your Estonian connections to use and get us more information on Baltic Invest. Tell your buddy on the force there that our killer might be Estonian; maybe some suitable candidate will come to mind."

"What about your brother?" Simolin asked uncomfortably.

"What about him?"

"How should we treat him?"

"The same as anyone else. Just do your job."

15

The Oxbaums lived in Lauttasaari, in a big, light-filled brick house. You could tell the place was no package design for the average homeowner; it was an architect's custom work that integrated the terrain and orientation. The picture window in the living room faced onto a view of a pine-dotted rock, and beyond that the sea. A view like that cost a nice chunk of change.

I had always considered Ruth a naive, almost pathetic figure, because she accepted Max's misdeeds with endless good nature and a hen-like maternalism. I had wondered on more than one occasion whether she was stupid, whether she was lying to herself, or whether she just didn't care. She had been a housewife for as long as I could remember. She didn't appear to have an iota of professional ambition, even though she had a master's degree in political science. Her ambitions were channelled into her home and her children – those arenas she had managed brilliantly. The house could have graced the cover of an interior design magazine any time.

I was surprised by how calmly Ruth was able to discuss Max's death, even though she had been a wreck the previous evening. Her sister was still there supporting her, and intermittently shot me cautionary glances.

"I'm sorry, I'm going to have to ask about some unpleasant matters."

"It's fine. I understand."

Ruth was leaning forward on the buttery-soft Italian leather sofa. Behind her hung an enormous abstract, an acrylic glowing in vivid yellows and oranges. With the dazzling autumn sun shining on it, it seemed to illuminate the whole wall. I recognized the artist, and guessed that the work cost as much as a mid-priced automobile.

"We're interested in knowing what exactly Max was involved in. No one is killed this way for no reason. Evidently he was in some sort of predicament. Do you know what it could have been?"

Ruth fiddled nervously with her wedding ring. Her fingers were long and beautiful, and Ruth wasn't bad-looking herself. She had a gentle domesticity about her. I could imagine her taking her prodigal, careworn husband into her arms and comforting him like a little boy who had cut his finger.

"As his wife, I suppose I should know. Unfortunately I don't, no matter how badly I wish I did. He had been acting strange for several weeks, letting trivial things upset him, but when I asked him what was wrong, he just put it down to pressure at the office."

"How did he react to Jacobson's death?"

"I could tell he was shocked, but he didn't want to talk about that, either."

"Are your financial affairs in order?"

Ruth looked almost offended. "Max handled them, and everything should be fine. I asked Max if that's what it was, and he said that the money was the last thing he was worried about."

"This is an expensive house," Stenman continued tentatively.

"Lawyers make a good living," Ruth retorted.

"Did Max have enemies, or did he ever mention having received any threats?"

"As far as I know he didn't have any enemies nor had he been threatened – at least he didn't mention anything of the sort."

"We have reason to believe he was being blackmailed, but why, we don't know. Money is the first thing to come to mind," I said.

"Don't lie to me. You know you believe Max was being blackmailed because of his other women," Ruth snapped.

"Did he have other women?"

"Of course he did, and you know it. But in their infinite wisdom, our mothers taught us that a smart wife turns a blind eye. Max knew that our marriage wouldn't have ended over something like that. That couldn't have been the real reason."

I struck an unexpected blow: "And what about you? Did you have other men?"

Ruth's breath seemed to catch for an instant, and she glanced at her sister.

"I don't suppose it makes any difference any more... I did, but only once. It happened last spring, when a friend saw Max kissing a young woman on the street. God knows how many times it had happened before, and I decided I'd get my revenge. You can be sure it had nothing to do with Max's death."

"Who was the guy?"

Ruth snorted glumly. "I don't think you want to know."

"Tell me anyway."

"Your brother. We screwed on the sofa in the office."

The word "screwed" sounded incongruous uttered by milk-and-cookies Ruth. It was even harder imagining her and Eli having wanton sex on the leather sofa where I had sat in innocent ignorance. I was a little shocked.

"Not money, not women – what's left? What about his reputation in the congregation? Could he have been blackmailed with, for instance, photos of a sensitive nature being sent to members of the congregation and his clients?"

"Blackmailed how?"

"Into providing information about Jacobson, for instance."

"I suppose it depends on the information. As an attorney, Max's reputation was important to him, but how important, I don't know. Do you think that Max had something to do with Jacobson's death?" Ruth asked, proving that she was anything but stupid.

"Max handled Jacobson's company's loans, and the company Max represented is suspected in Israel of money laundering. Max called Jacobson twice only a few hours before he was shot."

"Max was fond of old man Jacobson. He never would have got involved in anything that would have caused problems for him."

"Did Max ever mention Jacobson?"

"Nothing involving work. They were both on the congregation's board and met at each other's homes in that capacity. They didn't socialize otherwise."

"Did Jacobson come to the house?"

"Yes. Most recently, three weeks ago."

"What did they talk about?"

"I don't know. They were in the office. I went in to bring them coffee, but I didn't stay to listen. I imagined it had something to do with congregation business."

"More coffee?" Ruth's sister asked, filling my cup without waiting for an answer. Her cheeks were still burning from her older sister's revelation.

"And did Max ever meet Jacobson's son, Roni?"

"Why would he have?"

"Roni had also taken out a loan through Max."

"Max didn't care for him, and they had very little to do with each other."

"Why not?"

"I don't know. He spoke as if the company's troubles were the son's fault, not the father's. I thought it was unfair, because wasn't the recession really the underlying cause?"

"Did Max ever talk about the company he brokered loans for? The name of the company is Baltic Invest."

"No… or once he said something to the effect of it having been a mistake getting involved in the finance business. He didn't say any more, and I didn't ask."

"Do the names Benjamin Hararin or Amos Jakov mean anything to you?"

"Nothing. I've never heard of either."

"Is Jakov that Israeli billionaire?" the sister asked.

"That would be him."

"Why should I know an Israeli billionaire?" Ruth asked.

"He owns Baltic Invest, and Max met him when he went to Israel."

"Max didn't talk about his business affairs, because he knew I wasn't interested."

"And did Max ever mention Jacobson's daughter's husband, Joel Kazan?"

"Only that he saw him and Jacobson's daughter when he went to Israel. My understanding was that Kazan acted as a host of sorts."

Ruth's sister gave me a look indicating that it was time for the interrogation to come to an end.

"Max called me and asked me to come to the boat to talk to him. He promised to give me confidential information about something that would help me in my investigation of Jacobson's murder. That proves that Max was mixed up in the case somehow. When I went there, I found him dead. You do understand, don't you, that if you know anything about it, it's to your own advantage to tell me?"

Ruth looked at me coldly, but didn't respond.

"One more thing," I continued tenaciously. I had been wondering why Max warned me about buying a Benz SUV even though I had no intention of doing so. Had he been losing his grip and blurting out whatever popped into his mind, or did his words contain a message of some sort? "This may sound a little odd. Eli said that the last time he saw Max, Max warned me not to buy the same kind of SUV he drives, because it only gets a hundred kilometres to thirteen litres. I'd never mentioned anything to Max about buying a Benz SUV, nor did I have any intention of buying one. Why would he say that?"

Ruth looked moved.

"Maybe he was losing it… That's the only thing I can think of —" For the first time, Ruth's control failed her. She made a noise that sounded like the howl of a dog and then sobbed: "It would have been our twenty-fifth wedding anniversary next week."

16

I couldn't keep from swearing the moment we stepped outside. "Fucking Eli!" Stenman watched me, curious, but didn't interfere with my rant. I pictured Eli as an imbecilic little boy who was always underfoot, bouncing around as aimlessly as a pinball. It almost felt like he was making my life difficult on purpose: Baltic Invest, sex videos, an illegal weapon, and now screwing a murdered man's wife.

At the car, I paused for a moment and gazed out over the sea shimmering in the autumn sun. The northern wind already felt cold. I didn't understand why I had taken Eli's womanizing so seriously. Maybe as his little brother, I subconsciously expected him to act as some sort of moral example. My father had died when I was eleven.

"Do you want to talk?" Stenman asked, walking over to me.

"No thanks. I just want to get some fresh air for a minute."

A flock of barnacle geese flew southwards across the bay. I started thinking about what would happen if the birds didn't come back one day. Absurd. A criminal investigator who should be chasing a murderer is reflecting on the migrations of birds.

"All right, let's go," I said, climbing into the car.

"What was that SUV thing?" Stenman asked, once we were headed towards the Western Expressway.

"I think it was a clue Max left for me, even though I don't understand why he couldn't speak openly, why he had to drop hints."

"Has Oxbaum's car already been examined?"

"Forensics is working on it right now. Simolin and I took a quick look through it last night. I didn't find anything interesting except the pistol, which happened to be my grandfather's prize of war. It doesn't even have a permit. My best-friend's-wife-screwing brother gave it to Max because he was afraid of something. But Max didn't say what."

"Is that a bigger sin for Jews than it is for us Lutherans?" Stenman asked.

"What?"

"Screwing your friend's wife."

"Just as big."

"What's your relationship like with your brother?"

"Good, at least up till now. He could stop sabotaging my life."

Fortunately, Stenman didn't fixate on my revelation. She concentrated on driving, because we were turning onto the highway.

Once she found a gap in the lane headed downtown, she said: "There must have been something else in there, too. Parking stubs, unpaid tickets, stuff like that. There is in every car."

I remembered the receipts for coffee and gas from the service station. Max had purchased thirteen litres of gas...

"Thirteen litres of gas," I said out loud.

"What?"

"There was a receipt in the glove box showing that Max had bought thirteen litres of gas from a service station in Vantaa, and a receipt for coffee showing he had bought two cups of coffee, meaning he paid for someone."

"That's a strange amount," Stenman said. "Why would anyone buy so little gas for an SUV... unless you're buying with cash and that's all you have on you."

"It wasn't a cash receipt – it was a credit-card receipt."

"Do you remember the date?"

"I do, and the time, too."

I could tell Stenman was thinking the same thing I was. She beat me to the punch. "Why don't we head out there right now?"

The car had satellite navigation, so finding the place was easy. There were a few pumps under a canopy; behind them stood a tacky, boxy service station with an attached cafe. It didn't take long to find what I was looking for. The service station had a surveillance camera, or actually two. One was on the wall under the canopy; another was on the ceiling behind the register.

I addressed the twenty-year-old cashier. "I'd like to speak to the manager, please."

She pointed at a man who was stocking the shelves with multi-grade motor oil. I showed him my badge, and he dropped the oil for a second.

"What can I do for you?"

"How long do you keep the tapes from the surveillance cameras?"

"They're recorded on a hard drive, not tape. A month, unless there's some reason to keep them longer."

"We'd like a copy of a specific hour, to begin with."

"What hour?"

"1:30 to 2:30 p.m. last Friday."

17

It's hard to imagine a job that would give you such an intense feeling of success as being a police officer when the case you're working on starts to open up, especially if it's a violent crime.

The silent movies from the service station's surveillance cameras gave us just about everything we could have hoped for: the first role was played by Max, who drove up in his Mercedes-Benz SUV. He pumped the gas, moved the car and went inside. The interior surveillance camera showed Max pay with his credit card and walk over to the cafe, where he took a seat.

A moment later, a familiar blue Golf pulled up under the canopy. It passed the pumps slowly as if looking for the best deal, then turned into a parking space. The driver sat in his car for at least a couple of minutes before getting out.

Simolin, Stenman, Oksanen and I were glued to the monitor and the man approaching the camera. He was about six or seven yards away before he noticed it on the wall. He turned his head and passed the camera with his head tilted at a strange angle.

"Dammit, he noticed the camera," Stenman said.

"Didn't want to show his face," Oksanen continued. "Clear sign of guilt."

"Go back a little," I said, and Simolin rewound the recording. The image paused at the moment where the man noticed the camera.

He was about fifty years old, average height, slim. He had a light, relaxed stride. His hair was cut short, his face thin, his nose slightly hooked. The hook had been exaggerated in the sketch, so it was no wonder no one had recognized him.

Otherwise, he looked surprisingly similar to the drawing, down to the sunglasses.

Simolin read my thoughts. "It's the guy from the picture."

"If he's still in the country, we'll get him with that shot, that's for sure," Oksanen said.

"Fast-forward so we can see them when they come out," I said.

The meeting between Max and the man in the sunglasses lasted about twenty minutes. This time he was prepared. He exited looking off to the side, so his face wouldn't be visible. But the evasion came too late.

I called Huovinen, and he promised to come right over. Once he showed up, he looked at the still in satisfaction.

"Nice work. How did you find the place?"

I told him about the dated receipt we had found in Max's car.

"Does this mean that Oxbaum knew to anticipate his fate and left you a clue?"

"I think so. I'm pretty sure he left the receipts in the car so we'd find Jacobson's killer. Just to be sure, he told Eli to warn me against buying a Benz. He knew that by then at the latest I'd start wondering what he was talking about."

"Why didn't he just tell you?"

"For the same reason Jacobson didn't dare to reveal the person who was threatening him. Both were afraid that their loved ones would be targeted for vengeance. This way it looks like we got on the trail on our own – and we did, in a way."

I guess Max was smarter than I thought he was.

"What did the killer want from Jacobson and Max? What did they have that could have interested someone so much?"

"I'm not sure. It just occurred to me that if Jacobson didn't give the killer what he wanted, and neither did Max, will he move on to victim number three? It can't be about money, because Max definitely would have paid up if doing so would get him out of whatever mess he was in. "

"Could the motive have something to do with Jewishness after all?" Simolin asked.

Huovinen looked at me. "What do you think, Ari?"

"It's possible, I guess."

"Any other suggestions?" Huovinen asked.

"Maybe the killer's real target was some third party, say from the Jewish congregation, and the killer had been blackmailing Jacobson and Oxbaum for their help," Stenman suggested.

"Jewishness isn't the only thing Jacobson and Oxbaum had in common. Baltic Invest is another," Simolin noted.

I reconsidered the entire case, and for the first time I found a new take on it.

"We've assumed that the killer has something to do with Baltic Invest, because the Golf was owned by it and Jacobson's company's loan was from there. But we can also flip the idea around: Baltic Invest – or someone from there – is the killer's real target, and Jacobson and Max are only vehicles for getting at whoever that is. Max knew the owner of the company, Amos Jakov, and his frontman Benjamin Hararin. Jakov is originally from Russia; he has old criminal contacts there. He's also ex-high-level Mossad, and probably has plenty of enemies from those days. And then Jacobson's son-in-law Joel Kazan is a director at Baltic Invest."

"Not a bad idea," Huovinen said. "But that means the killer probably isn't Finnish."

"This guy looks Finnish," Oksanen said.

I continued explaining my scenario to Huovinen. "Hararin's companies have been investigated in Israel under suspicion of money laundering, but no conclusive evidence has been found."

"Could you put some more pressure on the police there for further information on the investigation? We could also send them that still to take a look at; the guy might be from Israel. In any case, we have something to work with now. Let's not release that photo yet, though, so we don't spook him. We'll use our own people to look for him first. Send that photo out to the patrols and warn them that they're not to attempt arrest. Nice work," Huovinen said again, before leaving.

As soon as the door shut behind Huovinen's back, Oksanen asked: "What about us?"

"Simolin, send the photo to the Tallinn police for identification. While you're at it, go ahead and send it to the Israeli police. Use Interpol. Arja, you email it to all investigators and patrols, and Oksanen, you and I will go show it to the neighbour who saw the gunman and the kids who found the car."

Stenman's eyes asked why I had elected to take Oksanen with me and not her. I had my reasons for everything.

It was my first ride in Oksanen's latest acquisition. Legally it was an automobile, but judging by the sound it was an earthmover.

"I changed out the engine chip, got fifty more HP just like that."

Out of politeness, I asked: "How much does this tractor get off the field?"

"About thirteen litres per hundred kilometres in the city; you can get down to about eight or nine on the highway. You have to be prepared to pay for your hobbies. Simolin has his redskins; I've got anything that rumbles and roars."

Oksanen was divorced and had a teenage son who was having discipline problems. Oksanen's interpretation was that the kid had been spoilt by his mother. The boy had already had a couple of run-ins with the police: once for theft, once for possession of a narcotic substance. "How's your son?" I asked.

"I sat him down for a serious talk, and I'm hoping he's finally learnt his lesson. Just to be sure, I made a deal with the warden at the juvenile prison out in Kerava that I can bring him in for a scared-straight visit whenever I want. He's a smart kid, but sometimes I think he's solid bone above the shoulders. Nothing sinks in."

*

Jari Wallius was standing in the road in front of his house when we arrived. He had heard us coming for blocks and was waiting to find out what kind of roadster was headed his way.

"Put on your tough-guy face," I told Oksanen as we stepped out of the car. In all likelihood, it would be our last chance to squeeze the kid for anything he hadn't told us yet.

"How many HPs does this have?" Jari asked, peering into the car.

"350."

"Wow… Dad's Volvo doesn't even have 200."

I handed the boy a copy of the print from the surveillance camera.

"This is the guy we saw," Jari said as soon as he saw the photo. "Is he the one who killed Mr Jacobson?"

I didn't answer. There were some things little boys didn't need to know.

"Have you remembered anything else? Anything you forgot to tell us last time we saw you?"

"No…"

Oksanen put on an intimidating expression, and bent down.

"You sure about that? You seem like a bright kid who notices all kinds of things other people don't."

"About the murderer?"

"About anything that might have to do with this murder mystery."

The boy thought for a minute and then tentatively said: "Could the other man have something to do with it?"

"What other man?"

"The one who came from the Jacobsons' back yard. He looked kind of suspicious and emign… enigmatic."

"When did that happen?" I asked.

"A little before we saw the guy with the car. When I took the shortcut to Sami's house, he was just sneaking out of the Jacobsons' back yard. Sami was still eating, so I had to wait for

135

him for a second. After that we went straight to the Seppäläs' yard to eat plums."

"So about twenty minutes before you saw the guy with the car?" I suggested.

"Yeah, about."

"Go tell your Mom that you're going over to the Jacobsons' with us."

"My Mom's not home."

The boy climbed into the back seat of Oksanen's car, his face beaming. A moment later we were at the Jacobsons' neighbours'. I asked the boy to wait in the car. The old man wasn't as certain, but said it was possible that the photo was of the impostor he had seen.

"Did you see anyone besides the policeman?" I asked the couple.

"I would have told you if we had," the man said.

We went back out and let the boy guide us to the spot where he had seen the other man.

"That's where he came from," Jari said, pointing at a spot where the hedge was thin. "And he went that way." Now he was pointing in the direction of the canal.

"And where were you when you saw him?"

"Over there."

It was about a hundred feet to where the boy was indicating.

"And you didn't see what he looked like?"

"He hurried by really fast, and he didn't look at me... Oh yeah, he had a hood on."

"What kind of clothes was he wearing?" Oksanen asked.

"Black – black sweatshirt and running shoes. He looked like he was out running."

I thanked the kid. It was time to pay a visit to Ethel and Lea.

"Can I get a ride with you guys?" the boy begged.

"If you wait in the car for a second," Oksanen promised. We walked around the yard and rang the doorbell. Lea opened the door.

I introduced Oksanen, and we stepped in. Ethel called down: "Who is it?"

"Ari… Ari Kafka."

Ethel hurried downstairs, and noticed Oksanen.

"Detective Oksanen."

"Did you catch him yet?" she asked, ignoring the introduction.

"Unfortunately not, but we've made progress. I'd like to ask you something. Is there a spare key to the house hidden outside somewhere?"

"Yes… or at least there used to be," Lea said.

"It's still there," Ethel said.

"Where is it?"

"In the back."

I asked them to show me.

The back door opened directly onto a patio furnished with a weathered porch swing and a set of silvery teak patio furniture. Lea took the key from a small terracotta pot under the stairs.

"I thought the murderer came in through the front door," Lea said.

"Probably."

We went back inside.

"Could you please take a look at this photograph?"

Ethel snatched the picture out of my hands and stared at it.

"Is he the one who killed Samuel?"

"Almost certainly."

It's rare to see such a primitive reaction. Ethel lifted the photo up to her face and spat on it.

"May he burn in hell."

That was a lot, coming from a Jew.

I took the picture and showed it to Lea. I saw her face grow rigid. Her eyes were nailed to the image.

"Have you seen him before?"

It took Lea a long time to respond. "Yes."

*

"Pull over somewhere," I said, once Oksanen was approaching Roihuvuori. "Let's think for a minute about what we've got."

Jari Wallius' revelation had shattered the picture that had been growing more and more complete: that the man whose face we had got from the surveillance camera and whose name we had got from Lea was the murderer.

Oksanen pulled into a parking spot next to the library. "Are you talking about how this second guy changes things?" he asked.

"That's exactly what I'm talking about."

"It might be something totally simple. There were two killers, and they were working together. One went ahead, the other one followed behind. Why didn't we think of that in the first place?"

"They were in the house at different times," I reminded him. "According to the boy, about twenty minutes passed between the visits."

"Kids that age don't have any sense of that kind of stuff."

"The boy said that after he saw the man in the hoodie, he went to his friend's a quarter of a mile away, and waited for him to finish eating and put on his clothes. From there, they went back to the house, which is another quarter of a mile. When the boys arrived, the man in the car was just leaving. It's only a minute's drive from the Jacobsons' to the other yard; it would only take a second to get the car into the garage, another couple of minutes to change clothes. Why would the killer have hung around for so long while the risk of getting caught was growing all the time?"

"Maybe he was waiting for his friend?" Oksanen suggested.

"According to the boys, the guy with the Golf was alone. The next question is, why didn't they leave together in the car?"

"That is weird," Oksanen said.

"And was the guy in the hoodie inside the Jacobsons' home? It would have been easy for him to enter with the spare key, but based on the patterns of the bloodstains, Jacobson was shot from the front, in the doorway to his home… And all the bullets were from the same gun."

"Where would he have found out about the key? According to the wife, only the family knew about it. Maybe the guy in the hoodie was some local prowler who happened to be on the property then," Oksanen said.

I stared ahead thoughtfully. "It's just that a man in dark clothes and a hood sounds a little too much like the guy who shot at me at Oxbaum's boat."

18

Agent Sillanpää from the Security Police and I were old acquaintances. At times it felt like he was having me monitored, because he usually showed up when I least needed it, making demands I needed even less. Like now. He was sitting on another chair in Huovinen's office, studying his knuckles as if he had just punched someone between the eyes and hurt his hand. And in a way, he had.

"Why can't we give the killer's photograph to the press?" I snapped.

Sillanpää dropped his still-balled fists to his lap. "Because doing so would endanger Operation Haemorrhoid."

I saw an expression cross Sillanpää's face that, if one were being charitable, could be interpreted as a smile.

"Don't let the name fool you. It's a major case, big-time. Its real name is Operation Jaffa, but the boys call it Haemorrhoid because we're watching a place around the clock and it's hard on the glutes."

"Is the target the same guy we're looking for in conjunction with the Jacobson murder?" Huovinen asked.

"He happens to be, unfortunately."

"What could be more serious than murder?"

"Two murders, or three, or even more. Taking him in now may have grave consequences."

"If we take him in, he can't murder anyone else," I said.

"Then he'll be replaced by someone else; someone whose name and identity we don't know."

"Who is the intended target of the guy we're looking for?"

"We don't know. That's the whole reason Operation Jaffa was set up."

"What exactly is it that you know, and why are you so sure he's intending to kill?"

"Tricks of the trade."

I considered what Sillanpää had said, and decided to pose a nasty question: "If you're been watching him for so long, how the hell was he able to kill Jacobson, and apparently Oxbaum, without you noticing? Is that a trick of the trade, too?"

"No, that was a lapse. But take into consideration the fact that the location is a difficult one to stake out with the resources at our disposal, and he's a professional. He's top of the line, Mossad-trained. It's hard to stay on his tail and…"

Sillanpää broke off and glanced at each of us in turn. "Everything I'm telling you stays in this room. Here's my offer. Kafka comes and works for us until this show's over. After that, you can do whatever you want with the guy."

"The guy named Leo Meir, formerly Vesa Nurmio."

Sillanpää looked at me, slightly surprised, but then he chuckled. "Looks like you've done your homework. I call him Nurmio; the Israelis can call him whatever they want. It's all the same."

"Then you'd better tell us the whole story," Huovinen said.

Sillanpää pulled a piece of paper out of his inner pocket, unfolded it, and handed it to me. "Sign here first."

"Do I get to read before I sign?"

"Knock yourself out."

The paper stated that I agreed to upholding confidentiality as outlined in such-and-such law, and if I violated the terms of the agreement, I could be convicted to a prison term of such-and-such length…

I signed.

"You could have consulted me before you did that," Huovinen said sullenly.

"This is the fastest way to move the investigation forward," I assured him, even though I didn't believe it myself.

"I don't think this is going to go on much longer. We've already been staking Nurmio out for over a month. He's too expensive a target to let dangle forever."

Huovinen cut to the chase. "You promised to tell us who Nurmio is."

"Kafka already knows."

"But I don't."

"Leo Meir, former name Vesa Nurmio, is a former Finnish citizen who has had previous dealings with the police, as the newspapers put it. In other words, we can call him a criminal without having to worry we'll be sued for slander. Nurmio checked out of Finland over fifteen years ago, around the same time the police were hunting for him on suspicion of felony battery and even more felonious narcotics violations. We didn't pick up his trail until a few years later, when he was living in Tel Aviv. And the next time he popped up, another few years down the road, he was already an Israeli citizen named Leo Meir."

"Why do you suspect this Nurmio of being here to assassinate someone?" Huovinen asked.

"Let me give you a little more background on Nurmio first, if you don't mind. The way Nurmio became Meir initially aroused quite a bit of speculation among us at the Security Police. We were sure that it all led back to Nurmio's past in the UN. In the '70s, he had served almost three years in the Golan as a young sergeant. During his final year there, he had been the commander's driver. According to Nurmio's UN buddies, he had spent a lot of time fraternizing with the Israelis. They suspected that he had cut some sort of deal with them. It was even alleged that he had taken care of some Palestinian activists for the Mossad; in other words he was a professional hitman. And apparently a pretty good one, because he was rewarded with Israeli citizenship."

"That was a while ago, though, right?" I pointed out.

"A lot has happened since then, it's true. Nurmio was transferred after knifing an Arab. Once his Golan gig ended, he spent some time in Lebanon and was involved in some dubious goings-on there. Then he came back to Finland, founded a car dealership, and lost it in a card game. He was subsequently linked to robberies of financial institutions, two of them, and to major narcotics deals, but no proof turned up until customs found two hundred kilos of hash in a German lorry. One of the guys who was arrested claimed that Nurmio had been the mastermind. That guy's brother was beaten to within an inch of his life. The witness recanted, but Nurmio still decided it would be best to disappear. And now he shows up again, but this time as Leo Meir."

"So what?" Huovinen asked.

"Nurmio owns an import company in Punavuori. We've been staking it out for over a month from the apartment across the street. He's not here to relive old times, believe me. He's here to kill. We received a tip that's so heavy-duty we can't afford to question it. The only problem is figuring out the identity of the person he's going to kill."

"But he already has killed," I reminded Sillanpää.

"That's just the prelude."

"What about Oxbaum?"

"That was the second act."

"But why did he kill those two?"

"Jacobson was a Jew, Oxbaum was a Jew, you're a Jew and you're leading the investigation. Which is precisely why we need you: to figure out why Jacobson and Oxbaum were killed."

"But you do have leads regarding Nurmio's next target, correct?"

"We do?"

"If Nurmio was planning on killing, say, an Estonian drug lord, why would you be interested? The target has to be political in one way or another."

Huovinen's eyes bored into Sillanpää. "Ari's right. Normal criminal investigations are our turf."

Sillanpää began waxing philosophical. "Who's to say what's political and what isn't? Sometimes it's a difficult line to draw."

"So teach us," I suggested. "Maybe we'll understand the difference."

Sillanpää continued as if he hadn't heard my gibe. "Let's assume that while he's in Finland, Nurmio kills, say, a Russian businessman who's a good friend and supporter of the Russian president and a former member of the Duma. That's already starting to tiptoe into our territory, because it can have ramifications on foreign policy and international trade. The Russians don't have much of a sense of humour when it comes to their citizens being killed on Finnish soil."

"Is that what you suspect?"

"It's one possibility. A man named Daniel Livson heads up Baltic Invest's operations in Russia. It's rumoured that he has connections to the largest criminal league in St Petersburg. We heard that he's coming to Helsinki some time soon. According to our sources, he knew Oxbaum..."

Sillanpää left the rest hanging in the air. That was clearly his tactic.

"And?"

"Livson is Jewish. From which some conclusions can be drawn..."

"Such as?" I asked patiently.

"I heard that Oxbaum and Nurmio met up not long ago at a service station cafe in Vantaa."

I glanced at Huovinen. He shook his head.

"Nurmio evidently had some hold over Oxbaum, and he may have demanded a service from Oxbaum in order to get close to Livson. Livson is in the habit of attending synagogue wherever he happens to be travelling. As his friend, Oxbaum definitely would have known when Livson would be on the premises. When Oxbaum refused, he had to be eliminated because he knew too much."

I was pissed off and didn't bother hiding it. "You guys know all that and you wait until now to contact us?"

"We each have our own roles to play, and our aims don't always coincide. Besides, this is all just conjecture. There is no evidence. It is possible that Nurmio isn't here for Livson after all."

"Let's assume he is. What's the motive? Why would someone want Livson dead?"

"We'll have to continue with the hypotheticals. Maybe he's trying to poach business from the Israelis and they decide they're not going to take it lying down. So they sic Nurmio on him."

Huovinen started looking perturbed, too. "If your source is so good, why don't they just tell you who Nurmio is hunting?"

"Even good sources don't know everything. We know Nurmio is here for something major, and Livson might be that something. The information comes from a friendly party who doesn't want Finnish–Russian relations to be endangered. And you can't demand too much from friends."

"Another country's intelligence service, huh?" I said. Sillanpää didn't respond, just stared ahead expressionlessly.

"And you're staking out Nurmio day and night for over a month simply because he *might* be planning on killing Livson? I have to say, I'm a little envious of your discretionary funds."

"Major impacts, major money."

"What about Jacobson?" I asked. "I'm sure you can provide us with a good theory as to why Nurmio killed him, and what that has to do with Livson's arrival."

"I think the reason for Jacobson's death is the same as for Oxbaum's. Nurmio blackmailed Jacobson first, but failed. Oxbaum was next on the list."

Something about Sillanpää's sudden generosity nagged at me, but I couldn't put my finger on what it was. "What good am I to the Security Police? You guys already know everything."

"We suspect all kinds of things – that's different from knowing. We want proof. For instance, information on what kind

145

of hold Nurmio had over Jacobson and Oxbaum, and if he can use the same ploy on anyone else. We believe the answer is going to be found among your people… I'm curious: How did you find out about Nurmio?"

"Jacobson's daughter IDed him from surveillance camera footage. They had attended the same party in Tel Aviv. Someone had mentioned to her that he was Finnish, and they had chatted. She remembered his name, too, Nurmio's Israeli name."

Sillanpää's interest was piqued. "What kind of party?"

"One thrown by her husband's employers. The employer happens to be the same company that owns Baltic Invest."

"Quite a coincidence. Or is it a coincidence?"

"I really have no idea."

"I'm assuming you milked the daughter for everything she had?"

"All she knew was that Nurmio lived in Tel Aviv, that he had received Israeli citizenship, and that he worked at the company as some sort of head of security. He reported directly to Hararin. That was the only time she met him."

"And I assume you told her not to discuss this with anyone, including her husband?"

"As a matter of fact, I did."

"Good job," Sillanpää said, as if he were a higher-up praising a subordinate. He stood and smacked his hands together. "So that's settled, then."

"When do I start?"

"Right away."

"So what exactly does that mean in practice? Will I be working from Ratakatu for the duration?"

"No need. All you have to do is keep us informed. We'll pass on more detailed requests for assistance as necessary. You can continue leading the investigation as you have been." Sillanpää eyed me for a moment, then continued: "And the most important thing is to not do anything that would endanger our operation. So the photo is not going to the press. Is that clear?"

He stood to leave.

"Sit down," I said. "One more thing. Even though you seem to have good informants inside your unit, you don't know everything. The ballistics tests for the bullets that killed Jacobson and Oxbaum just came in. They were fired from the same gun."

"Yeah, I thought that was understood."

"That's what I thought, too. It's just too bad that the man who killed Oxbaum on his boat and fled by kayak wasn't Nurmio, or even Meir."

19

When it came to the affairs of Finnish Jews, I had an advantage, and not simply because of my background. I'm referring to the fact that my uncle Dennis was the first one to hear about anything that happened in the community. He was one of the congregation's most liberal supporters, and all doors were open to him. It was high time to pay him another visit.

He lived alone in a large apartment in Töölö. It was surrounded by parks, and had a view of the Rowing Stadium and the sea. A museum-like stillness prevailed inside, even though details revealed that a living family had once resided there. That family had dwindled as one of Dennis's sons died of a drug overdose, his daughter moved to Stockholm, and the second son to Israel. His wife had died over ten years earlier. The deaths of his son and wife had struck a deep wound in my uncle's soul, but he had engaged in a long, grim monologue with God and they had come to an understanding.

My uncle had suffered a severe heart attack early that summer, and as a result had been spending more and more time alone by choice. He told me that he wanted to reflect on things in peace. I still visited him a couple of times a month, and phoned him more often.

I was fond of my uncle. He had helped Mom out after Dad died and lent her the money to buy a hair salon. He was the only one of my relatives who had supported me when I had applied to the Police Academy.

My uncle was sitting in his patinated club chair like Marlon Brando in *The Godfather*. He was wearing a light-blue plaid shirt under his V-neck sweater. Despite his casual dress, my uncle radiated an uncommon dignity, and his soft, wandering gaze could sharpen bright and diamond-hard at any moment. He knew I was there on business. A steaming cup of tea stood on the cigarette table. After his heart attack, he had hired an elderly housekeeper. She had carried in tea and sandwiches for us.

"All right, let's have it."

I protested innocence: "Let's have what?"

"The question you want to ask."

"We'll have time to get to that."

"But I'm not just impatient, I'm also curious."

"It has to do with Jacobson's death... and Max's."

"I heard about Max. He's the last one I'd have expected... I mean that he'd get himself killed. I was certain that with all those extra pounds and cholesterol levels like that he'd die of a heart attack or a stroke. I suppose my heart attack didn't ask what my cholesterol levels were, though. Which, if anything, taught me that I'm mortal, too. Somehow I'd managed to forget. I'm sorry, go on."

"I believe that the murders are not only linked to each other, but to something else, something bigger. One possibility is that Jacobson was first pressured into getting involved in something. After that, the killer came after Max, and I'm afraid that won't be the end of it. The killer needs help, and he's looking for a new helper."

"So the killer must have had some sort of hold over Jacobson and Max?"

"So it would seem."

"Then it must have to do with Max's business dealings. I've always suspected that they wouldn't stand the light of day. I warned your brother, but evidently he didn't listen to his uncle."

"That's what I think, too. Max had brokered loans for Jacobson's company. The lender was an outfit named Baltic Invest."

"I'm familiar with it. I can't imagine ever being desperate enough to borrow money from them."

I believed my uncle. On the other hand, it was easy for him to say. His financial affairs were more than in order. He had been a bank director for over thirty years, and in addition was a partner in a successful investment company. I was certain that he had a seven-digit account balance; in other words, four digits more than my own. I hadn't inherited the knack for money-making that was considered the birthright of every Jewish boy.

I had thought on many occasions about how different brothers can be. My father was the scientist type, a humanist and a nature lover. He was more at ease during his work trips to Lapland than he was in his own home. My uncle, on the other hand, was an urban, cigar-smoke-scented businessman down to the tips of his fingers. He had softened with age, but I still couldn't imagine him walking down a hiking trail in Lapland or binding birch whisks on the sauna steps.

"When he was in Israel, Max wandered off the straight and narrow, and someone videotaped it. He, at least, was being blackmailed with those tapes. Samuel Jacobson was probably being blackmailed with something else, but what that was, I don't know. I don't even have a good guess."

My uncle listened, apparently absent-mindedly. But I knew he heard every word, including the ones I left out.

"Samuel intended to pay off that loan. He came here to discuss the matter, and I gave him some advice. Despite the fact that things weren't going quite as well as they had in the past, his company had considerable assets. So it can't have had anything to do with the company's loan."

"His son Roni's loans were also arranged through Max. He took out loans totalling almost a million euros."

"Still."

"You know that Jacobson's daughter Lea is married to the Israeli director of Baltic Invest. Maybe the killer threatened to do something to them?"

My uncle's hands started to tremble as he sipped his tea. This was due to his age, though, not the topic of conversation.

"Did Jacobson offer any reason as to why he intended to pay off the Baltic Invest loan?" I asked.

"He had heard that they were under investigation in Israel. He thought there was something fishy about the company. He was angry with his son-in-law because he had recommended a loan from them even though he was perfectly aware of the scandal."

"Did he use the word 'angry'?"

"No, but it was clear from his tone. He told me he had read his son-in-law the riot act, and also spoken to his daughter about it."

"What feelings did he have about Max's role in the matter?"

"He was irked about that, too. He felt that Max just skimmed off his share and bore no concern or responsibility for the company's credibility. Max had boasted about what a financially solid company Baltic Invest was. Samuel said that he had given Max a piece of his mind, and your brother, too, even though Max was the one who handled all the loans."

"Did Roni intend to change lenders, too?"

"We didn't discuss that."

"What's your opinion of Roni?"

I valued my uncle's knowledge of human nature. As a bank director, he had learnt to assess people's character. I remember him telling me that not a single one of his customers had skipped out on a loan. Or one had, but he had a good excuse: he was hit by a car and died.

"Roni is the type who tears down everything earlier generations have built up. There's no way he would have ever been a director if he hadn't been Samuel's son. Samuel would also bemoan Roni's tomfoolery from time to time."

"What did he mean by tomfoolery?"

"Oh, most recently he'd complained about the affair… When Roni started seeing that former beauty queen."

"So it wasn't about money or anything more serious?"

"If it was, he didn't tell me."

"You said that the company's loans couldn't have been used to blackmail Jacobson… But what if Roni had screwed up his finances, and that was used to blackmail his father? How do you think Jacobson would have reacted to that?"

"He would have cleaned up the mess, or at least helped Roni clean it up."

"What if the mess was too big to be cleaned up with their money?"

"Then it would have had to be a truly massive… How would Roni have ever achieved anything of that scale?"

"I don't know, but I know there are plenty of ways. Some guys are gamblers, some make bad investments, others take drugs. Roni was in Lapland when his father was shot. One possibility is that the father knew of the threat and sent his son away to safety. He locked himself up in the house and told everyone he was sick."

"Is that what you suspect?"

"It's one possibility that occurred to us."

"Have you interrogated Roni?"

"No, we've talked to him, that's all. We don't have any evidence of anything like what I just mentioned. Other motives could exist. Does anything else occur to you?"

My uncle leant back in his chair and let his head fall back until his gaze hit the spot where the ceiling and the wall met. It was his typical stance when he was concentrating. It was his way of shutting himself off from the outside world. I let him think in peace.

"Is there room for the victims' Jewishness in your theories? I'm not talking about the most obvious thing, anti-Semitism, but something related to our community. Could that be the factor linking the two cases?"

"That occurred to us, too, but we couldn't come up with the link."

"How about the Jewish congregation? Jacobson was on the board."

"But not Max, at least as far as I know."

"No, but he was on the congregation's security committee ever since your brother resigned."

"That's not much of a coincidence. Any congregation member who's the least bit active is invited to take a leadership position."

"It's only been a month and a half. Your brother's resignation was unexpected."

"Do you know why he resigned?"

"Because of time commitments, evidently. I heard that Silberstein was a little peeved. Max stepped in for him."

I hadn't heard about this, but I wasn't too up on goings-on in the congregation. I only attended synagogue on the most important holidays, like Yom Kippur, which was coming up way too soon.

"What do you know about the killer?" my uncle asked.

I broke the Criminal Investigations Act by revealing confidential information to him, but with my uncle I knew that I'd get my investment back in spades. Furthermore, I trusted him. He would never do anything that would put me in a compromising position. I told him everything, down to the surprise visit from Sillanpää.

"That's quite the quandary you're in. You could have excused yourself from the case because of Eli, and Lea too."

"I didn't want to, at least not yet. If anything else comes up, I guess I'll have to."

"More coincidences. The presumed killer is working for Baltic Invest. Your friend at the Security Police suspects that the killer is here in Helsinki to assassinate a Russian criminal while he attends synagogue. That sounds believable at first, but when you start thinking about it, it doesn't. Not really. In the first place, why kill someone at the synagogue? It's not the easiest place for an operation like that. The synagogue will be monitored and guarded, and making a getaway would be difficult. It would be a lot easier to kill the Russian somewhere else. Let me show you something…"

My uncle rose, retrieved a folder from the glass-fronted bookcase, and handed it to me. It contained press clippings from an Israeli newspaper, some in Hebrew and others in English. They were about Amos Jakov, who was considered one of the wealthiest men in Israel, and delved into the criminal investigations focusing on him and Benjamin Hararin.

"I've been keeping up with the story purely out of my own interest," my uncle said.

"I heard that the investigations had been called off," I said.

"That's true. But they might be starting up again. It all depends on one man."

"Who?"

"Don't you follow events in your spiritual homeland? The Israeli Minister of Justice resigned four months ago, and the new Minister of Justice has announced that the affair will be investigated down to the very bottom. He's a dangerous man; evidently he's so insanely honest that he intends to expose his experience and knowledge of bribes involving politicians from his own political party. He has already revealed how the Mossad sold information gathered through wiretapping to businessmen, and how they made millions off it by buying or selling stock at the right time. One columnist wrote that the new Minister of Justice is so principled that he can look forward to a very short life."

My uncle's story sparked a vague memory that I sensed was somehow important, but I couldn't get a proper grip on it.

"Who is the new Minister of Justice?"

"Haim Levi. Former secretary of the Labour Party. He has held prominent positions in the party for almost fifteen years. Levi also knows about the Mossad's doings, so they don't have a lot of love for him, either."

"Haim Levi," I repeated, as I remembered where I had heard the name. He was the young man posing with his host in the photo in Samuel Jacobson's office. The former exchange student had metamorphosed into a man of influence. No wonder Jacobson had hung the picture on his wall. I doubted it had been there before Levi's advancement to power player.

I told my uncle about the photo. He furrowed his bushy brows and gazed at me, almost in wonderment.

"So now do you understand?"

"I'm not following…"

"Levi will be paying a visit to Finland soon, and Samuel was one of those responsible for planning the agenda. Last time we met, he said that Levi had announced that he wanted to go and relive old times at their cottage. He was an exchange student here, and stayed with the Jacobsons. My guess is that the target is not some Russian mafioso, it's Levi. And my guess is that your friend at the Security Police knows it, too."

20

It was starting to feel like, in addition to keeping tabs on me, Sillanpää always tried to screw me over whenever I ran into him. My instincts told me that my uncle was right and that Levi was the killer's true target. But in spite of the political dimensions, Sillanpää's deception felt too egregious. I asked myself what he imagined he was achieving by sending me after some Russian mafioso. Then I answered my own question: he was afraid I would arrest Nurmio before they had accumulated sufficient evidence that he had been hired to kill Levi. If that were the case, Sillanpää had, strictly speaking, told the truth. And it was presumably also true that he wanted to exploit my connections to the Jewish congregation. I had to admit that the mafia man thing was a pretty clever ruse. While Sillanpää was sending me off on a wild goose chase, the information brought in by my investigation would help them crack the Levi case.

I decided that he wanted to hide the true target because it involved foreign policy and the delicate relationship between Finland and Israel. Anything of the sort was too sensitive to turn over to normal criminal investigators. Such matters were hallowed to the Security Police.

After reflecting on it, I eventually decided to see how things progressed without revealing my suspicions to Sillanpää. I'd borrow a page from his book, and bluff.

I decided to start by making the rounds of the bigwigs in the Jewish community. In a sense I had already begun with my uncle and brother, but now I'd step outside the family. I chose Silberstein as my first target.

I didn't beat around the bush; I went straight to his workplace. He was upper management at a large engineering firm, where the lords of millimetre-precision machining and the princes of stress calculations sat in meticulous, modest cubicles staring at their computer screens, as if all earthly wisdom were contained therein.

Silberstein glanced at me with his usual coolness, and I felt like a corporate spy from Apple in the holiest of Microsoft holies. The room as was drab as every other one in the building. Silberstein was no visual maverick. He probably wasn't a maverick in any sense of the word. The bookshelf held company publications, patent legislation and a few other deadly boring yet appropriate volumes. A couple of corporate pennants stood on the windowsill, and a large photograph hung from the wall. It showed Silberstein shaking hands with a guy with a moustache. I took a closer look and realized it was Olympic swimmer Mark Spitz, who had won seven gold medals for the US in Munich. Spitz was Jewish.

"Was that taken in Finland?" I asked, genuinely curious.

"No, Jerusalem. Would you mind getting to the point?"

The fact that Silberstein didn't even try to impress me by telling me more about his meeting with Spitz revealed the caste to which he relegated me.

I replied equally brusquely. "I'd be happy to. To begin with, could you tell me what duties Max Oxbaum had in the congregation?"

"What do you mean... what duties?"

"He was on the executive committee. Did he have some particular area of responsibility?"

"Yes. Security." I didn't laugh, even though I found this amusing. Max's role in the congregation wasn't news to me, but it offered a good entrée to the real matter at hand. "He took over when your brother quit."

"What did that mean in practice?"

"He represented the congregation and worked with the security company, the police and the security detail from the Israeli embassy as necessary, considering the risks represented by various events."

"Jacobson and Max were both on the executive committee, and now both of them are dead. Has that occurred to you?"

"At least not from the perspective you're getting at."

"And what perspective would that be?"

"Isn't it obvious? That their position in the congregation would have been the cause of their deaths."

"Why couldn't it have been?"

Silberstein's response was a dispassionate stare tinged with a pinch of condescension.

"Did Max have anything out of the ordinary going on right before his death?"

"What do you mean by out of the ordinary?"

"Did the congregation have any risk-sensitive events coming up where Max would have been involved in the arrangements?"

Silberstein hesitated for a second. When he continued, I knew he was lying, or at least soft-pedalling.

"No, nothing out of the ordinary."

"Hmm. That's strange. I heard that Haim Levi, the new Israeli Minister of Justice, would be visiting the synagogue during his trip to Finland. Has the visit been cancelled?"

This time Silberstein thought for at least three seconds. "There has been some correspondence about the matter, but —"

"But what?"

"He has preliminarily promised to attend, but —"

"Don't you find the visit worth mentioning?"

Silberstein pouted.

"Did Max have anything to do with the visit?"

"He had been in touch with the ministry, but —"

"I don't want to hear any more buts, just the facts."

Even Silberstein leant back when I raised my voice. I was a criminal investigator, after all, and had all of the authority bestowed by my office behind me.

"I can hear perfectly well without you shouting," Silberstein said, his voice dripping indignation.

"You're sabotaging the investigation by holding back critical information."

Silberstein's face darkened storm-black. Before long, lightning would strike. "Now you're going too far. You can be sure that I'll speak to your superior about this. You've underestimated me badly. The chief of staff at the Ministry of Justice is a good friend of mine —"

"Why don't you just talk to me instead? Max was in charge of arranging the minister's visit, and you didn't say anything about it. You also didn't say anything about Samuel Jacobson being involved in the arrangements, and to top it all off, that he knew minister Levi. We're trying to come up with a motive for Jacobson and Max's deaths, but you're holding back information. Why?"

Silberstein struggled with his outrage for a moment and then said, in a surprisingly compliant tone: "There's no proof that the murders are related to the visit. The last thing I want to do is spread rumours that would hurt the congregation."

"They *are* related, and you know it full well. Were you afraid the visit would be cancelled if there was some remote chance that risks were involved? That the congregation, or you, would forfeit an amazing PR opportunity, and you'd lose out on a new photo op that would look great hanging there next to Spitz?"

"What have I ever done to you? You're intentionally trying to offend me. The Israeli Ministry of Justice is aware of what has happened. We were also informed in no uncertain terms that the unfortunate incidents that have taken place here will have no effect on Levi's visit."

"Not even the agenda?"

"We haven't been informed of anything of the sort, at least."

"Jacobson knew Levi personally. Levi lived at his home during his year as an exchange student. Isn't that true?"

"So I was told."

"Was Levi supposed to visit Jacobson at his house?"

"No, at…"

"At?"

"At his cottage. Levi had such fond memories of the place when he lived in Finland that he wanted to visit there again, to go for a sauna and a swim."

"What about now that Jacobson is dead? You just told me that there weren't going to be any changes to the agenda."

Silberstein stared out of the window. A busy arterial ran past, and more dreary grey element-construction buildings stood on the other side of it.

"Samuel's son Roni has promised to act as host during the visit to the cottage."

"At Emäsalo?"

It wasn't really a cottage, but an old farmhouse on the sea. The sauna was right at the waterline. I had been there with Lea once. After bathing in the sauna, we had skinny-dipped under the August moon.

"And are you participating in this jaunt to the cottage?"

"That was the plan."

"Who else is going?"

"Of the trustees, myself, Josef Mayer and Jari Kantor; and then Roni, of course, and his friend Dani Pasterstein, who also knew Levi; Joel Stern, and your brother Eli."

I felt a twinge in the pit of my stomach.

"Why is Eli going?"

"He returned to Max's place on the executive board. He's taking over Max's duties during the visit."

21

If Eli had been a little tipsy the last time we met, this time he was dead drunk. And he didn't even try to hide it. When he tossed soil onto Max's coffin, I was afraid he would fall into the grave. I could see the tears stream down his cheeks, even though he clumsily tried to wipe them away.

"*Barukh atah Adonai Eloheinu melekh ha'olam,*" Eli mumbled in Hebrew. It meant: *Blessed are you, Lord, our God, sovereign of the universe.* After that, he tore so violently at the collar of his shirt that his top button flew into the grave. Rending one's clothes was part of the Jewish burial tradition, but Eli's interpretation was in a class of its own.

He had started drinking before Max's funeral, and started right back up after the ceremony, out of a pocket flask. Some of the attendees eyed him in amusement, my uncle Dennis in concern and Silberstein in disapproval. Silberstein's expression augured a short career for Eli in the governing bodies of the Helsinki Jewish congregation. This time, none of the glares had any effect on Eli. He could be thick-skinned, especially when drunk.

After the funeral, I offered him a ride, because he had come by taxi. I wanted to get him home as directly as possible.

"No chance, little brother. I feel like stretching my legs."

He shambled off, reeling like a sailor headed towards a ship waiting at the docks. I played bodyguard and shadowed him. The first signs of autumn were already showing in the cemetery. Some of the flowers were starting to wilt, and a few yellow leaves could be spotted in the birches. The sun was shining from the direction of Kaivopuisto, giving off a pleasant warmth.

Eli stopped and, leaning against a large oak, lowered himself to the grass. He took another swig from his pocket flask and offered it to me. I sat down next to him and wet my whistle on his cognac. Two days' worth of stubble shadowed Eli's cheeks, and there were stains on his white shirt.

"Are you wondering what happened to your brother, since he's looking so much the worse for wear? I'll tell you. The last time I was at home was the day before yesterday, and I haven't changed shirts since then. What would Mom say if she could see her son now?"

Mom wouldn't say anything, I thought. She would have just got a good grip on Eli's hair, dragged him to the tub and scrubbed him with a hard brush till his skin was raw. Mom had always preferred action to words. The fact of the matter was, though, she was also perfectly capable of tossing barbs so sharp that their target felt like a dartboard. I had put my mind to it, but I couldn't remember a single tender word ever having passed Mom's lips.

"I'm not wondering what happened to you. I'm wondering what's happening to you."

"Well, what do you think? Let's hear your analysis, Sherlock Holmes."

"At least Silberstein didn't care for your little show."

"Good. Silberstein can kiss my ass. He's nothing but a pompous old scarecrow. I've had it up to here with his bossing me around. The old fart thinks he's Moses reincarnated, leading his people to the Promised Land."

"I'd rather talk about you and Max."

"Leave poor, dead Max alone. If he fucked up, he took responsibility for it. There's not a whole lot more you can do, is there?"

"Responsibility for what?"

"I wish I knew. Max is six feet under now. That pretty much put an end to everything, so why don't we, too?"

"You know I can't. The investigation is still ongoing."

"Baby brother. I'm going to tell you to your face that you don't know what you've stuck your big fat nose into. You're like a flyweight in a heavyweight match. That always ends badly. Here, have a swig." Eli shoved the flask into my hand again.

I handed the flask back. "The fight's not over until the last round. Besides, I'm fast on my feet."

Eli looked at it and said: "Do you want to hear why I'm drunk?"

"Because you feel guilty that you went and screwed Max's wife, on the sofa in your office no less, and it's too late to ask for forgiveness."

The flask paused on its way to Eli's mouth. "She told you?"

"Who else?"

"Why would Ruth tell you that?"

"Because I asked her."

Eli glared at me accusingly. "You fucker. Why'd you have to go and ask her about stuff like that?"

"How could I have known what you and Ruth had been up to? I just asked a general question."

Eli shook his head and finished taking the swig. "You're right. I feel bad about that too, but right now I'm mostly drinking because I'm so fucking afraid… And because I'm mourning what happened to Max. Max could be annoying and smug, but he had his good sides, too. You don't know about them. To you Max was just a clown: Maxwell Smart. You're the one who came up with that name."

"What are you afraid of?"

An inquisitive squirrel circled down the trunk of a tree and bounded onto the grass. Eli held out his flask to it. The squirrel eyed it in an evaluative manner and twitched restlessly, as if unsure of what he was supposed to do with it.

"Would you care for some Hennessy XO, Mr Squirrel? XO means extra old. The best that money can buy… and there's more where this came from."

Eli pulled a flat half-litre bottle of cognac from the pocket of his trench coat.

"No? Squirrels sure are picky these days… When I was a little boy, squirrels ate whatever they could get their hands on. Those were the days of the post-war shortage, though… What am I afraid of? I can't tell you, otherwise you'll be afraid, too."

"Try me."

"No way. I don't want to get you mixed up in anything, even though you seem to be getting me mixed up in just about everything. You are my baby brother, after all, despite the fact that you're a fucking cop and you have the soul of a boy scout."

"You've already mixed me up in whatever it is, whether you like it or not."

Eli jabbed me in the ribs with an outstretched finger. "I don't have anything to do with that… Max did, unfortunately. He paid a high price for it, the highest imaginable, even though I warned him a lot of times. Why the fuck did he have to be so cocky?"

"Are you talking about Baltic Invest?"

Eli grunted, but didn't answer. "You cops are always so fucking nosey. Why? Tell me why. Is it something you're born with?"

I knew from experience that Eli could be hard to manage and irritating when he was drunk, so I proceeded with caution. He was already so agitated that he was saying whatever popped into his head.

"Do you know who killed Jacobson?"

"You guys are the ones who should know."

"If I tell you that we do know, what would you say to that?"

"Ari. Ever since we were kids you thought you were smarter than me, but you're not."

Eli leant back against the oak's rough surface and closed his eyes.

Slightly modifying the truth, I said: "We know who killed him. The killer is a criminal named Nurmio, who now goes by Leo Meir. He works for Baltic Invest. He needed Jacobson's help and tried to blackmail him. Jacobson refused, which is why he was killed. I'm sure that Nurmio or someone else was also blackmailing Max."

Eli kept one eye closed, and for a second I thought he had passed out. He eventually continued: "So you're sure. Well, go on then."

"We believe that Nurmio is in Finland to kill Haim Levi, Israel's new Minister of Justice, who has ordered the Hararin and Jakov investigations reopened. You know that Levi is coming to Finland in a few days."

Eli cracked open both eyes warily, as if the light pained him.

"Have you noticed that there are lots of gorgeous women in Tel Aviv? Too many. Fuck! And you think you're being careful," Eli said angrily. He took a long swig from the bottle.

"I already know that you and Max were being blackmailed about women."

"It's thousands of miles away. For once you think you can have a little fun without someone you know coming out of the woodwork right when you're feeling up a blonde."

Eli's words would have amused me if Max weren't dead and he wasn't in such bad shape.

"There were no blondes in Tel Aviv, even though I said there were… no, no one was using women to blackmail me, because my wife doesn't care, believe it or not. Max, on the other hand, thought that his wife never noticed anything, but she noticed everything. Ruth told me that she knew about Max's flings, but didn't want to make a big deal about them. Pretty civilized… Let's not make a fuss out of this. But Max went all soft because he was afraid the photos would be sent to Silberstein and the rest of the conclave and they'd be posted online and he'd be a laughing stock. He was jiggling like a bowl full of Jell-O."

Eli tried to laugh, but his laughter turned into a nasty-sounding snort.

"Has Nurmio been in touch with you?"

Eli put his forefinger to his mouth. "My lips are sealed."

"Is he blackmailing you with something besides women?"

This time Eli didn't even listen. "Max was my best friend."

I shook Eli by the shoulder. "You're drunk, but I still want you to tell me what Nurmio wanted from Max. We believe Nurmio is going to try and blackmail some third person next. Is it you? Is it Roni?"

Eli tossed the empty bottle into the bushes and popped open the second one.

"Why did you go back to the congregation and rejoin the executive board?"

"Someone had to do it… 'Before them lay the bog… rough boards bridged the mire… they crossed them through the fog… to the hut, humble and dire…'"

Eli leant back against the tree and appeared to fall asleep. I shook his shoulder harder.

"Eli, you can't pass out there."

Eli opened his eyes. "Who's passing out? I'm just resting my eyes. You can keep a lookout to make sure no one steals my wallet and my Amex Gold or my Rolex, which is not actually a cheesy Rolex but an elegant Patek Philippe. But before that, there's one thing I want to say, then I'll shut up. You guys are so fucking wrong, you have no idea."

"What about?"

"Meir or Nurmio or whatever his name hasn't killed anyone. He's here for totally different reasons…" Eli closed his eyes again, and a barely audible murmur slipped out between his lips: "…there they bore the farmer's lass…" Then he started to snore.

I shook him by both shoulders. "Eli. You can't pass out here." This time he didn't react.

There wasn't anything I could do except wait. I decided to give him half an hour's grace. Then I'd wake him, even if it meant dumping a bucket of water over him.

I made myself comfortable and turned my face towards the sun.

It looked like it had fallen to me to be my brother's keeper.

22

"Nurmio's gone," Sillanpää said the instant we met. He had called me at work and asked me to come right over to the site of the stake-out. "He disappeared last night, probably through the basement, and we haven't seen him since."

I looked around the apartment from which Security Police agents had been monitoring Nurmio's doings for over a month. I wondered whose name was on the lease and who paid the rent.

The place was a one-bedroom flat on the third floor. It was furnished as spartanly as possible; there were no unnecessary comforts. That might have encouraged slacking. The only furnishings were a couple of chairs and a table, on top of which lay a laptop and a black notebook. All events of interest were logged in the notebook, along with the time. The kitchen contained a microwave, a coffee machine and a fridge. A digital video camera on a tripod stood at the window, with a SUPO agent sitting at it.

"Pretty lousy stake-out if you didn't notice anything," I remarked, taking a look through the camera.

Sillanpää walked over to where I was standing at the window. He raked his fingers through his greasy hair and left it sticking straight up. Then he pointed across the street. A hard rain was whipping the city and the window, blurring the view. Thunderstorms had been forecast for that evening. Autumn had arrived in Helsinki.

"I wouldn't say so. Nurmio's place is in that building diagonally opposite. Tough floor plan. There's a back door in the stairwell that goes to the basement, and from there routes lead in all kinds of directions – including the back yard and the courtyard of the building next door. We had one vehicle parked outside, prepared to follow if Nurmio made any moves. During office hours, we'd get a couple more too, but do you think we have the resources to watch every single escape route and rat hole? We're already cooking the books to stretch our budget."

"What are your plans regarding Nurmio?"

Sillanpää walked into the kitchen and took a paper mug from the table. "You want some coffee?"

I nodded, and Sillanpää poured some for me. I sipped it. It was old and strong. Coffee like that kept agents alert during their shift. I dropped in a couple of sugar cubes and stirred it with a plastic spoon. Sillanpää tapped two sweeteners into his cup.

"You wouldn't believe how many packs of coffee we've gone through in a month, and how many kebabs and pizzas. The restaurant's probably going to go out of business once surveillance ends. I wonder how they'll claim those kebabs on expenses? Probably the bosses' entertainment account."

"Have you started looking for Nurmio?"

"All the places we know of: former girlfriends, criminal buddies, his sister who lives in Vantaa. Nothing. It's a tough manhunt, because we can't ask directly. We don't want him to find out about us."

"You'd think he already had."

"There's nothing to indicate that. We believe he went underground because he saw a drawing of himself in the papers. So thanks a lot. I'd be grateful if you had something in your back pocket that would help us find him. We've got so much political pressure on us that we're starting to split at the seams. The Minister of the Interior knows about this and his calcified veins are about to pop."

Regardless of how he was talking, Sillanpää didn't appear particularly stressed.

"Has he had any visitors?"

"Over the course of the stakeout, he only had four visitors, three of whom were women. Nurmio brought them home from a nightclub and they disappeared within a couple of hours. Boom-boom, bye-bye. We stopped them and told them we were narcotic agents. None of them knew Nurmio from before. They just left with him since he lived nearby and was pleasant company. None of them had been given his phone number. All he had told them was that he sold Israeli boat and car chemicals and had lived in Israel for a few years."

"And the fourth?"

Sillanpää gazed out at the rain sweeping the street as if he found the natural phenomenon truly fascinating. "It's raining pretty hard… The fourth was Max Oxbaum."

Sillanpää saw my face, and could tell I was seriously ticked off.

"Sorry. We hadn't agreed on cooperation at that point. Now I'm playing with an open hand. Oxbaum came here two days before he was killed. He came in the middle of the day and was inside for twenty minutes or so."

"I suppose you talked to him, too?"

"He was an attorney and a sly old fox. We decided it was wisest to not expose ourselves."

And now I decided it was time for me to show my hand.

"That story about a Russian gangster visiting Finland was a complete fabrication. You said you were playing with an open hand."

Sillanpää knew how to maintain a poker face. "Says who?"

"You think Nurmio is here to kill the new Israeli Minister of Justice, Haim Levi, who is coming to Finland in a week."

Sillanpää considered this for a moment. "All right. Open hand. We didn't want to tell you about Levi, because we suspected that your brother was involved. We do believe that Levi is the target, but we don't suspect your brother any more."

"Why not?"

"Something turned up."

There was no point pressing him. Sillanpää wouldn't give me anything more about Eli. On the other hand, what he had told me put my mind at ease.

"Max must have been in touch with Norm. We could compare his telecommunications data with Jacobson's."

"Good. Do it."

"Who paid the rent on his place?"

"Nurmio paid half a year's rent in advance. The money came through an Estonian bank, a former shell company. Oxbaum bought it three months ago and is on the board. Nurmio's name doesn't appear anywhere."

"I'm assuming you guys tapped Nurmio's place?"

"No. There was a deadbolt. We decided it was best not to try so we wouldn't tip him off. Mossad training means noticing visits like that."

"Regardless of whether or not Nurmio had Mossad training, there's no point waiting around any more. Let's go over and see what we can find."

"You think so?"

"Yup. There must be some clues in there."

The thought clearly appealed to Sillanpää. "I have to talk to my boss." He went into the kitchen and made a call. I waited at least five minutes, listening to a hole being drilled into the wall in the next apartment over.

"They've been remodelling for two weeks," the agent at the camera said.

"You guys only have one man staking out at a time?" I asked.

"At first there were two of us, but we used up our overtime pretty fast, so we had to scale back to one."

Sillanpää returned from his expedition to the kitchen. "OK. We're good. Our lock guy will meet us there."

"What about me?" the agent asked as we were leaving.

"You stay here. Warn us if you see him approaching, even though I doubt he's coming back."

We waited outside for the SUPO lock specialist to arrive. Once he got there, we negotiated in the car for a minute and then decided to go in through the back door. To get to it, we had to head around to the back and down to the basement. We stopped at a grey door. The door had two locks: a normal house-key lock and a Boda deadbolt. The Boda looked brand new.

Sillanpää gave the order: "Go for it." He had promised we didn't have to worry about leaving signs of a break-in; the main thing now was getting the door open. Calling in the building super would have required too much explaining.

The specialist drilled a hole an inch in diameter between the locks, at the point where the door and the jamb met. He slid in a crowbar. One powerful wrench, and the door popped open.

Sillanpää peered in. He didn't see anything, so he continued in. I followed.

The back door opened onto a hallway with a bathroom off to the side. That led to an unfurnished back room and the street-side storefront, where the large display window had been covered with blinds.

The main room contained a desk, a couple of armchairs, a computer, an almost-empty bookshelf and a dead body. It was lying on its back near the middle of the floor, its half-open eyes staring blankly at the ceiling. A pistol with a silencer lay next to one hand. There was a bullet hole right under the eye, another in the temple.

"Don't touch anything," I instinctively ordered Sillanpää. He stopped and looked at the body.

"It's not Nurmio."

I had noticed the same thing. The deceased looked like a foreigner.

I bent down and went through his pockets. The wallet held a driver's licence issued in St Petersburg. According to it, the man's name was Igor Semeyev.

"Russian."

"He has a gun, too. What the fuck happened here?" Sillanpää growled.

"Probably what it looks like. There was a shoot-out, and Nurmio shot our friend Igor Semeyev here."

"No wonder Nurmio split," Sillanpää said.

23

I was sitting at my window, watching flashes light up the southern sky somewhere above Suomenlinna. I counted the seconds: one, two, three, four... ten. A scattered rumbling rolled between the buildings and deepened to a drum-like thud.

Ten times the speed of sound in a second. The thunderstorm was two miles away.

I had always liked storms and thunder, but only on land. They scared me at sea. When we were kids, Dad would take us to down the Kaivopuisto marina, where the waves would crash onto the rocks and the wind would hurl salt spray in our faces. Dad had loved it, too. Eli, on the other hand, had always been terrified of storms and thunder. He'd drag his feet and shriek until Dad would be forced to lug him down the shore. Things like that had to leave indelible trauma.

The wind rattled the open ventilation window, and the raindrops pelted my face. The sensation of water and wind felt like a caress from Mother Nature.

My beautiful scheme, which had been based on Nurmio's culpability, was completely demolished, and I hadn't managed to piece together a new one in its place.

The dead body that had been found in Nurmio's room had been confirmed as the person indicated on the licence. The St Petersburg police had corroborated his identity. He was a criminal that the Russian police were more than familiar with, a paid hitman for the Minsk mafia. It was a pretty sure bet that he was also the man I had seen at Max's boat, as well as the one Jari Wallius had seen leaving the Jacobsons' house.

After receiving this information, it felt like I was trying to put together two different puzzles whose pieces had been scrambled up. No matter how hard I tried to fit them together, I couldn't form a picture that made any sense.

Was the mafia killer after Nurmio, or vice versa? Or had they been working together and then argued about something? When two killers argued, more often than not dead bodies would result.

Semeyev must have entered through the back door, because the SUPO stake-out man hadn't noticed him. I almost felt sorry for the guy who had been on duty at the time.

Nurmio presumably knew Semeyev, because he had let him in. The gun we had found at Semeyev's side had been fired once. A .22 calibre bullet was found in one of the cupboards in the kitchenette. It had pierced the door and bored into the back wall. In addition to being the right calibre, Semeyev's gun was the right make, a Margolin. It looked like Semeyev had killed both Max and Jacobson.

The bullets that had killed Semeyev, on the other hand, had been fired from a 9 mm.

Sillanpää had been just as mystified as I was. On top of it, he cursed the fact that Semeyev had been shot while SUPO was staking out the premises. That wouldn't look good in the reports, especially if it got leaked to the press.

A huge bolt of lightning lit up the sky, and the thunder followed only a few seconds later. The thunderstorm was right overhead now. It was like the sky was pummelling the city in its ribs. Rain drummed against the windowsill at an ever-intensifying pace, and the wind picked up until the large linden in the courtyard of the building opposite was forced to bend to it. A woman was running down the street with an umbrella, trying to get into her portico. The umbrella turned inside out from the force of the wind. She found her keys and dove into the shelter of the stairwell.

Like a lot of old-fashioned people, Mom had been afraid

of thunderstorms and had rushed around unplugging all the appliances as soon as she heard any rumbling. She told us stories from her childhood of lightning balls entering a home through the telephone, circling the room and exiting through the window…

My cell phone rang. I glanced at the screen: blocked.

"Is this Detective Kafka?"

"Who's asking?"

"Someone you've been pretty eager to find these past few days – at least according to the papers."

"Nurmio?"

"No, Leo Meir. I've already got used to my new name. Are you interested in meeting me?"

"Why? I'm not —"

"This is an offer that will not come again. Do you want to meet me or not?"

"Of course —"

"Good. Where are you?"

"Central Helsinki. Punavuori."

"Good. Then fifteen minutes is enough. Does your phone have enough battery?"

I glanced at the power symbol. Four bars. "Yes."

"Keep your phone on the whole time so I can hear you. Put on a warm coat and head towards Iso Roobertinkatu. Do it now… And leave your gun at home so there aren't any accidents."

I followed his instructions and at the same time wondered what I should do. I didn't have a landline and couldn't call anyone; besides, Nurmio would have heard me. I walked down the stairs and out of the door, headed left and, at the next intersection, turned onto Fredrikinkatu. The wind was blowing from behind me, from the sea, and I took shelter between two buildings. The rain had eased off a little.

"Where are you?" Nurmio asked.

"Freda."

"Good. Tell me when you're at the corner of Iso Roobertinkatu."

That didn't take longer than a minute. "Now."

"Continue towards Bulevardi."

I followed his directions.

"Turn onto Uudenmaankatu," Nurmio said, and a moment later added: "And take the next left onto Annankatu."

I had almost reached Bulevardi when Nurmio said: "Stop."

I stopped and looked around.

"Turn back."

I turned and walked back towards Iso Roobertinkatu.

"Stop. There's a silver Opel station wagon in front of you. Get in on the driver's side."

I saw the Opel. It was parked in front of an antique shop. I could see someone sitting in the passenger seat.

I looked into the car. I had no problem recognizing Nurmio. He was wearing a dark sports coat and a burgundy tie. He pointed at the driver's seat. I paused for a moment, then made my decision. I opened the door and sat down at the wheel.

"Pleasure to meet you, despite the fact that I'm not a big fan of the police. Start up the car, and we'll go for a little drive."

I started up and headed towards Bulevardi. I slowed down as we approached the intersection, and Nurmio immediately told me which way to go. "Take a left... If you know who I am, why haven't you told the press? No decent picture, not even a name, even though you have both."

I didn't answer.

"It's all the same. I didn't ask you here to answer my questions, but to listen."

"Suits me."

"I didn't kill Jacobson, so you're looking for the wrong guy."

"Who did, then?"

Nurmio grunted. "Don't underestimate me. I noticed that you guys have already paid a visit to my lodgings. You found the answer there, didn't you?"

"Igor Semeyev?"

"He's a killer for the Russian mafia. You ran tests on his gun, didn't you? It was probably used to shoot Jacobson and Oxbaum."

Nurmio was right. The gun had been fast-tracked through the tests, and it had been confirmed that it had been used to shoot both Jacobson and Oxbaum.

"And you shot Semeyev?"

"I had to. The shithead tried to shoot me, and he almost didn't miss. We've known each other for years, but it just goes to show you can't trust anyone."

"Why did he try to kill you?"

"Someone had given him orders. Semeyev doesn't kill for fun."

"Who is the someone behind the orders?"

"Stop for a second."

I found a parking place off of Hietalahdentori Square.

"I'm not sure, but I can offer you a few good candidates. I've been making some calls and poking around since I killed Semeyev. I'm starting to get to the heart of what's going on. I think you'll be interested in hearing what I have to say."

I admitted I was. "Can I take notes?"

"Go for it. You've probably looked into my background. What do you know about it?"

"You were suspected of narcotics violations and —"

"I mean the period when I was in the Middle East," Nurmio said.

"You're suspected of having done favours for the Mossad, because you received Israeli citizenship so quickly."

Nurmio laughed.

"You could say that again. I did them a lot of favours: big favours. I saved the Mossad a lot of headaches."

"And now you're working for a company owned by Benjamin Hararin. And Hararin in turn works for Amos Jakov."

"Also true. Good. Nice to see someone do their homework properly. Jakov and I met when he was still in the Mossad. I was his subordinate and carried out his orders. He's an intelligent man; I'm not at all surprised he made a fortune in business. He had old criminal contacts in Russia, and he used all the knowledge a high-level Mossad leader has to his advantage, and that's saying a lot. He's so rich and powerful these days that no one sneezes in Israel without him knowing it. Ten years ago, I was conducting some business of my own in Syria and Lebanon and doing a few favours for Jakov on the side. When I got back to Israel, he hired me to work for his company, in security."

"Is he the one who sent you to Finland?"

"In a way."

"If you didn't kill Jacobson, what were your orders?"

"To remind him, Oxbaum and a few other people that they owed certain parties a debt of gratitude. They were starting to forget. I was also supposed to ensure that they behaved themselves and didn't cause any trouble."

"What trouble could they have caused? Are you talking about the Baltic Invest loans?"

"So you know about them, too. You've been busy. Oxbaum was awarded the Finnish loan business because he knew Hararin's business partner. He arranged a loan for Jacobson and saved his son from personal bankruptcy and forfeiture of assets."

"Roni?"

"Beautiful women and expensive tastes can be a dangerous combination."

"Did the father know about it?"

"He didn't hear about it until a few weeks ago."

Nurmio eyed me. "I think it's time we started talking about what we could give each other. I can give you information, but what would I get in return?"

"The police don't bargain…"

"Too bad for you."

"…but I'll listen to anything you want to tell me."

"That's starting to sound better already. I didn't kill Jacobson, although I know it looks like I did. And that's because that was the intent. Someone wants to frame me as the culprit. As soon as I realized that, my eyes were opened. I was led like a lamb to the slaughter, but not any more. The first thing I want is for you to take my story into consideration, and not believe everything they're trying to get you to believe. The people behind this know what they're doing."

"That's an easy promise to make."

"Maybe, but I have no intention of coming down to headquarters and telling you this on tape. I had my fill of prison in my past life."

"I can't promise that you won't be arrested. You admitted to shooting Semeyev. Even if it was in self-defence, something like that can't be overlooked."

"What if I can prove that Semeyev tried to kill me? OK, he's a killer and he had a gun, but I'm no Boy Scout either. That means jail time, at least with my background, even though I'm actually a pretty nice guy."

Nurmio glanced at me. A smile flickered across his face, but vanished just as quickly.

"If you can prove the threat, it will be interpreted as justifiable self-defence."

Nurmio didn't appear to be listening. "I have a nice home in a place where oranges grow. The climate in Finland is horrible and the food disagrees with me. I find all of that depressing. I'll help you however I can, and then I'll clear out of here and spend the rest of my days keeping my nose clean and browsing the Catechism. How does that sound?"

"I can't promise —"

"That's what I thought. You Finnish cops are such choirboys. In Israel, we know how to cut deals. The Jews are a trading people. You must be the exception who makes the rule."

"It would help you if we knew who Semeyev was working for and we were able to get proof that he killed Jacobson. The neighbours saw you at the scene of the crime."

"I know. I was wondering why they wanted to know so damn precisely what time I would be going to see Jacobson. Because I was being framed as the murderer."

"Why did you go there?"

"Like I said, I was trying to put his mind at ease so we could discuss things like civilized people. He thought I was a killer, and didn't dare to meet me. I couldn't come up with anything else. Now I see that the other side scared him into locking himself up at home."

"Who wanted to know about your visit?"

Nurmio laughed. "We'll talk about that later."

"What about Max Oxbaum? We have surveillance camera footage of your meeting."

"Was it from a service station in Vantaa?"

I didn't answer. "Why did you two meet?"

"I needed Oxbaum's help. At the same time, I was trying to get him to understand that he'd better leave Baltic Invest alone, or at least not go around blabbing about its affairs. It wasn't an easy balance to strike. Kind of the same thing as with Jacobson."

"You needed help? With what?"

"OK. I think it's high time I let you in on something that might take some pressure off you."

Nurmio reached into his pocket and handed me a plastic card. I turned on the light in the sun visor and inspected it.

"Are you telling me that you're still working for the Mossad?"

"Isn't that what that says?"

That's what it said. There was also a photo on the card.

"I'm here on a job that seems to have gone totally fucking haywire. Now you can stop worrying and listen to what I have in mind."

I opened the window and inhaled the brisk sea air to clear my head.

"Shoot."

24

I had to admit that Nurmio's revelation took me completely by surprise. Even though the card looked genuine, I couldn't shake off my disbelief.

"If you want, you can call my boss in Tel Aviv and check it out. Contact is only allowed in emergencies, but I'm pretty sure this counts as one."

"Let's forget that for now. You'd better just tell me what this is about and what you want."

"All right. Why don't we agree that you don't take notes after all? I'm here because the Mossad and the Israeli police are jointly investigating Jakov's connections to organized crime and the related bribing of officials. I was asked to infiltrate Jakov's organization, and two years ago I managed to get back on his payroll because I'd known him in the past. I told him that I'd got the boot from the Mossad a long time ago and had been conducting some business of my own in Syria and Lebanon. Which I had, but that had been part of the cover."

"It's a long way from Tel Aviv to Helsinki."

"Which is why they needed me, and why I was ordered to help the Israeli police. It's a small world. You see, it so happens that there's a man on Jakov's payroll named Joel Kazan. Kazan is married to Jacobson's daughter. Through his brother-in-law Roni, Kazan met Max Oxbaum, who was eventually given Finnish representation of Baltic Invest."

"Why specifically to Max?"

"He was greedy enough and had good contacts. And initially Max handled the business pretty well, but little by little things started getting out of hand. Max started using quite a bit of coke, and the business suffered. He brokered a large loan for Roni when Roni divorced his wife and built a new house by the sea. Roni simply didn't pay it back. A few other loans also generated large losses. Israel finally had enough and sent Kazan in, because in a way he was responsible for Oxbaum. Jacobson didn't care for his son-in-law, and when he told him about Roni's loan, Jacobson said it wasn't his problem; why had they been so insane as to go and give Roni a personal loan?"

A police car drove past slowly. Nurmio watched it. Once it had turned at the next intersection, he continued: "Kazan had prayed that Jacobson would take care of it, because Jakov had said that Kazan could kiss his life goodbye if he didn't fix things. I guess Jacobson didn't want his daughter to be a widow. In his panic, Kazan got drunk and said more than he should have. He told Jacobson that Jakov was a criminal and that Baltic Invest was laundering money. He imagined that Jacobson would get scared, or at least take pity on him. Bullshit. Luckily for us, things just got worse. Jacobson responded curtly and said he knew the Israeli police were investigating Hararin's and Jakov's affairs. He threatened to report Baltic Invest to the authorities. Another factor played a role in this, which proves how small the world truly is…"

I digested Nurmio's story. It seemed incredible, but true. And I couldn't think of any reason why Nurmio would lie.

Nurmio sized me up, as if trying to assess whether what he had told me had made the desired impression.

"How does the story continue?"

"Israel got a new Minister of Justice four months ago. The new Minister of Justice, Haim Levi, had made a lot of noise about exposing official corruption and gutting criminal organizations, especially Russian ones. Levi had spent a year as an exchange student in Helsinki in the 1980s. And lived where else but…"

"…at the Jacobsons'."

"Exactly. And Minister of Justice Levi was coming to Finland for a visit and intended to meet up with his former host family. When Jacobson heard about that, he got what he thought was a brilliant idea. He informed Israel that he intended to tell the whole story to his old friend, Minister of Justice Levi."

"And you were ordered to kill Levi?"

Nurmio laughed.

"That's what the Finnish Security Police thinks," I said in my defence.

"I know. They were watching me from that building across the street 24/7 for an entire month."

SUPO's operation was starting to look like a total farce. A month of completely pointless work.

"Someone has supplied them with false information, and not by accident."

I was intrigued. "Who?"

Nurmio looked sincerely amused. "It feels like a stunt we would pull. They couldn't set one of their own on him in a friendly country, so they put SUPO on the case and let them pay for the stakeout and handle the reporting. I'd bet that they've asked for regular reports on my doings either directly or through the CIA. If I get a warning for fucking on the job, at least I know where the information came from."

"Are you saying that none of these events have anything to do with Levi's visit?"

"I never said that."

"Both SUPO and I have a stake in Levi's visit. It would be pretty bad advertising if the Minister of Justice were killed while he was in Finland."

"Whoever said that he's going to be killed? Let me finish. Jacobson was in contact with Levi and announced that he could help him investigate Jakov's business affairs, because he possessed incendiary information about Baltic Invest. Furthermore, he went and said that Max Oxbaum could provide inside details on the company's operations and deliver documents if the Israeli police would protect him from Jakov. This is the point when I enter the picture. I wanted them on my side. It just so happened that Jakov sent me – who else? – to Helsinki to clear up the mess because I'm a former Finn. I was supposed to put the screws into Jacobson and frighten him into silence; or at least that's what Jakov said. Of course I was in contact with Jacobson, because I wanted to hear everything he knew. Like I said, he got scared because he thought I had been sent to kill him, and barricaded himself in his house. I met Oxbaum, who was also suspicious because he knew I worked for Jakov. I couldn't reveal my mission to them right off; I had to proceed cautiously. I was already making inroads with Oxbaum, and everything was going pretty smoothly until Semeyev showed up. He went and killed Jacobson and Oxbaum, and pinned both murders on me. It's hard to do your job when the cops are breathing down your neck and your face is plastered all over the television and the papers."

"Do you mind telling me already what Levi's visit has to do with all of this?"

"It confirmed for Jakov that Jacobson was serious and intended to tell everything. Since Jakov didn't know what that everything was, he didn't want to take any risks. The fact that Jacobson was Kazan's father-in-law made the risk that much greater. Jakov suspected Kazan of having blabbed too much to his father-in-law. Oxbaum didn't know much, but whatever he did know was too much. Together Jacobson and Oxbaum presented such a major risk that it was easier just to get rid of them."

"How did Jakov find out about Jacobson's intentions?"

"You're still not getting it. From Levi himself. The Minister is one of Jakov's men. All the talk about rooting out corruption is a pile of horseshit. The whole point is to use Levi to smooth things over in Israel. The journalists trust him as if he were some new prophet, and the investigation couldn't come to a close until the journalists had given their blessing to its conclusion. That's why Jakov paid Levi more than anyone else. He's our second prime target, and he's the reason I'm in Finland. Semeyev was sent here to clean up the mess before Levi arrived. They used a Russian just in case he got caught. An Israeli killer would have pointed in the wrong direction."

"Levi is still coming, and is meeting Jacobson's son Roni. They're going to the Jacobsons' cottage."

"I know all about the visit to the cottage. I'll get back to that in just a minute."

"Did Roni know that his father's life was in danger?"

"I don't think so. He promised to pay off his debts as soon as he became CEO. I heard him suggest to Kazan that the old man should be given a little scare, be intimidated into retiring. I'm sure he understands that everything is interrelated."

"Why did they want to get rid of you?"

"There aren't many alternatives. Either Jakov has figured out that I'm still working for the Mossad, or he just wanted to get rid of me and make me the scapegoat for the murders of Jacobson and Oxbaum while he was at it. That would be just like him."

"What happened at your place?"

"Semeyev called and announced he was coming by because Jakov had ordered us to work together on a gig. He came over and said that Jakov was losing his patience with all the shit that was going on in Finland, and that the whole mess had to be cleaned up for once and for all. That's when he pulled out his gun and fired. Luckily I was ready for him and managed to take cover in the kitchenette. He missed, I didn't. I left the body and the weapon behind so you could figure out the truth."

"How are we going to prove that you acted in self-defence and that Semeyev also killed Jacobson and Oxbaum? Maybe the gun is yours and you put it in the deceased's hand after you shot him."

"That's easy." Nurmio pulled a small digital recorder out of his pocket and handed it to me. "Give it back after you make a copy. I recorded Semeyev's call and the entire shoot-out. Every second is on that tape. If I'm not completely misunderstanding things, I'm an innocent man."

The amount of information Nurmio had given me was making my head spin. "Let's assume I believe you. Where do we go from here? Regardless of what happens, I have to tell my superiors about this."

"That's fine. But if it's all the same to you, I'm not prepared to meet them; at least not yet. There's still time to turn things around to our advantage if we cooperate."

There was one question that had been going through my head for a long time. Now it was high time to ask it.

"My brother Eli was Oxbaum's business partner, and travelled to Israel with him. What do you know about him?"

Nurmio was quiet for a moment. "I knew your friend Dan Kaplan, and I know what happened here two years ago. It was not to our credit or to Kaplan's, even though he was a good man. He and I had been in a lot of tight spots together. Dan must have told you what Oxbaum and your brother got up to in Israel."

"A little."

"The investigation was already underway then, but that just goes to show what a difficult case this is. Wrenches are being tossed into the works from every side, and you bump into enemies no matter which way you turn. In Israel, these things aren't as simple as they are here in innocent little Finland. One of the things Dan was supposed to do was to get Oxbaum and your brother on our side. He began to spend too much time playing one game and was careless in the other. The fact that your uncle shot him in front of the synagogue on Yom Kippur carries some pretty heavy symbolism. It even made the papers in Israel. Dan called me from here a couple of days before he died, and told me he was in a moral conundrum. He was supposed to try and use his childhood friend – in other words, you. You can count it in his favour that he took pleasure from it."

"I was asking about my brother."

"He helped us; he convinced Oxbaum to work with us. We don't have anything against him."

"I don't understand why he would have helped you."

"Let's just say he realized it would be mutually advantageous. Dan's groundwork didn't go to waste. It'd be better for your brother to tell you about it if he feels like it."

Nurmio unrolled the window and stuck out his head. "The thunderstorm passed." He extended a hand. "It was nice meeting you, but I have to be on my way."

I stepped out of the car and watched Nurmio drive towards Ruoholahti. I walked across the windswept square towards the shore where the sea surged, tamed by the harbour's breakwater but still daunting.

I needed some time to think before I called Huovinen and Sillanpää.

I was sure the thunderstorm hadn't passed yet.

25

A man should trust his instincts, at least sometimes. I had never liked Roni, and now I was sure that my instincts were right. He didn't deserve anyone's regard; he was a total shit. It was just too bad that criminal law didn't mention anything about being a shit.

I told him I wanted to speak to him again, as new information had arisen in the investigations of his father and Max's murders. He tried to ask what, but I just told him when we expected to see him at Pasila for his interrogation. I reassured him just enough that he didn't have the sense to bring a lawyer along.

He arrived at the agreed time in the afternoon. I led him into a conference room. I brought Simolin and Stenman with me.

As soon as he sat down, Roni tried to lighten the mood. "The way you were talking, I was wondering whether I should call my lawyer friend and bring him with me."

"What would you have needed a lawyer for?"

"Nothing. That's why I didn't call him. What new information are we talking about?"

"Just a second," I said, jotting in my notebook. It was just nonsense words. Men like Roni got nervous when you ignored them.

"All right. We're recording this conversation," I said, and Simolin turned on the recorder.

Roni wasn't able to keep a look of concern from flashing across his face.

Once again, he tried to lighten the mood. "Do all three of you really need to be here?"

"Max's murder forced us to change tack in the investigation and reconsider motives."

"Why are you worried about motives? You have a murderer. His photo was already in the papers, right?"

"Very probably, but it's not certain yet."

"Come on, you guys don't put a photo in the papers unless you're positive."

"We're simply looking for him on suspicion of committing a crime," Simolin said.

"We already know who he is, and we'll be apprehending him soon. But even if he were the perpetrator, he must have been working for someone. We want that someone, too."

"Who's the guy in the picture, then?"

"A former Finnish criminal who has received Israeli citizenship. He's violent and dangerous. We know he's suspected of several assassinations. Another reason the motive is so critical is so we can try to predict his next moves."

"If he's a professional, he's probably not hanging around Finland waiting to get caught."

"We believe that he hasn't carried out his primary mission yet. We need your help to figure out what it is. That man is genuinely dangerous, not someone you just find and bring in. He has already killed three people."

"If I knew anything, I would have told you... Wait, who's the third?"

Stenman took the lead. "We can't reveal that at this point... We suspect that the real motive might have something to do with your father and Oxbaum's roles in the Jewish congregation."

"What roles?"

"Your father was involved in arranging the new Israeli Minister of Justice's visit to Finland, and so was Oxbaum. It's possible that the killer tried to get information on the visit from them. That means that the target would actually be Levi."

"That also means that he might try the same thing with a third individual privy to the visit's arrangements and Levi's schedule," I said. "Which includes you."

All three of us looked at Roni. It must have felt uncomfortable.

"Do you guys really suspect that Dad's killer tried to get information from me about the visit?"

"You know Levi because he lived with you as an exchange student twenty years ago. I heard that Levi wanted to relive old memories and go for a sauna at your cottage. Is that true?"

"Yes, but... goddamn it. Believe me, you guys are way off here. Why would anyone want to kill Levi, and here in Finland of all places?"

"Because he has threatened to expose corruption and collusion between politicians and criminals. Killing Levi here is a lot easier than in Israel. Plus you can always pin the blame on some crazy anti-Semitic Finn."

Roni was clearly rattled. "I don't know what to say... or what I can do to help..."

"Were you aware that, according to telecommunications data, your father was in contact with the Israeli Ministry of Justice on numerous occasions?"

"So what? It must have been to do with the visit... I mean, I know it was to do with the visit, let's put it that way."

"It's also possible he wanted to tell Levi something about, say, Baltic Invest. Something he might have heard from Max."

"Why the hell..."

I glanced at Stenman, and she took the floor. "We've been in touch with the Israeli police and we know that Levi's revelations would specifically threaten Benjamin Hararin, the owner of Baltic Invest, and Amos Jakov, whose front man Hararin is considered. Your father and Oxbaum may have had information that would have been dangerous for him."

"Just a second ago you were suspecting that my father was killed because he didn't provide information about the visit, and now you're claiming that Dad and Max were Levi's sources."

"True," I said. "But they might be interrelated. Let's assume your father found out something from Max, something of a sensitive nature about Baltic Invest. Can you guess what it might be?"

"I have no idea... I can try and think. If I come up with anything I'll be in touch right away..."

"We'd also like to know more about your personal connections to Baltic Invest," Stenman said.

"There aren't any."

"We understood that you borrowed money from them."

"That can't be considered a connection. Thousands of other people have, too."

"Who arranged the loans, Max or your brother-in-law, Joel Kazan?"

"Max did, of course."

"What is the total amount of those loans?" I asked casually.

Roni sprang up. "My personal finances don't have anything to do with this. If I had known that the interrogation was going to sink to this level, I would have brought along a lawyer to ensure my rights."

"We make the decisions about what's relevant for the investigation. Believe me, we're not asking out of curiosity, so sit down," I ordered him. "The sooner you answer the question, the sooner you'll get out of there."

"A little over a million."

"So you have loans in the amount of a little over a million euros?" Stenman repeated.

"Yes."

"Those are some pretty substantial monthly payments. Several thousand euros, off the top of my head."

"I can handle them."

"Especially now that your father is dead." My remark was a cruel one, I had to admit.

Roni latched on to my words. "What are you implying?"

"That your stake in the company increased and you became CEO. I assume that also meant a raise."

"I would have become CEO anyway."

"But not as soon as you wanted to be." We sat quietly for a moment, faces grave. Then I continued: "Since you and I know each other, I'll tell you frankly that we were seriously considering arresting you, so we could have some time to investigate your company's loans and personal financial affairs. However, we decided at this point to give you a chance to answer all of our questions as a free man. We hope cooperation will go a little more smoothly in the future."

Roni rushed to assure us: "Of course I'll help you any way I can. I don't have anything to hide."

"Will you show him out?" I said to Simolin.

Once the door had shut behind Roni, Stenman said: "We were pretty mean to him."

"He deserved it."

"Do you think he'll pass the word on?"

"I know he will."

26

Autumn put her best foot forward as we wound our way through the southern Finnish forest. Now and again, a vista of rolling pastures and idyllic farmhouses would emerge behind the trees. This was a prosperous region, one whose residents hadn't had to resort to eating pine-bark bread during the shortages. In the rays of the autumn sun, the world was awash in vivid green and yellow, like a Van Gogh painting.

The Jacobsons' cottage was an old log-framed villa on the seashore. The property included a woodshed, a tool shed and a sauna painted traditional farmhouse red. The latter almost hung out over the water, and the sea lapped at the stone foundations of its porch.

Sillanpää was about a hundred yards away, his binoculars trained on the sauna. Nurmio was examining his cell phone. A rifle equipped with silencer and telescopic sight balanced on a bipod on a nearby rock.

"I never would have imagined in a million years that I'd be involved in anything like this," Sillanpää said. "I should be protecting Levi, and instead I'm giving a Mossad killer a shot at him – and to top it all off, on purpose."

"I'm the one taking the risks, and you guys will win out," Nurmio promised generously, as he had before.

Sillanpää's superior had been in touch with Nurmio's boss at the Mossad, who had confirmed that Nurmio was on a very important clandestine mission and requested he be given any support possible. The assignment demanded exceptional measures, even according to Mossad standards, but in this case they were up against exceptional forces as well.

Sillanpää had been given almost free rein, as well as freedom to take responsibility if something went awry and the affair resulted in a diplomatic incident. I had spared Huovinen's civil servant morality from being stretched beyond its limits and given him the light version of my involvement.

Even though Semeyev had been confirmed as the murderer, the crime wouldn't be solved until the person who had ordered the hit had been taken into custody. I told myself that I was still working towards that. And I was.

"Now," Sillanpää said softly.

Three men stepped out of the sauna with towels around their waists and beer bottles in their hands. They sat down on the sauna terrace.

"I think it's time to make the call," Nurmio said, more to himself than us, and started tapping at his phone. A moment later, I saw my brother Eli come out of the sauna with his phone. He handed it to one of the men sitting on the terrace. The man looked at the phone, perplexed, but then lifted it to his ear. The 15x zoom on my video camera served me the cottage as if on a platter.

"Hello, Minister Levi. It's me, Leo Meir. Do you remember me?"

Nurmio was standing right next to me, and I could hear every word.

"Hi, Meir. I don't mean to be rude, but I'm in a pretty tight spot here, so if you don't mind, let's talk later —"

"You have no idea what a tight spot you're in, Mr Minister."

"I'm afraid I don't understand."

"You're in Finland, on the terrace of a sauna. The sea looks gorgeous today."

"How do you —"

"Because I can see you and I'm aiming a rifle at you. Do you mind stepping off a little to the side, so we can talk privately? A few feet is enough…"

Levi looked around, stood slowly, and walked to the end of the terrace. He gestured at the other two men, indicating that he wanted to talk privately. They rose and went inside.

Nurmio's polite tone instantly turned into brusque orders.

"Good. Now listen to me. I'm caught in a nasty bind. The Finnish police are hunting for me for the murders of Samuel Jacobson and Max Oxbaum. In addition, a Russian killer tried to shoot me. I'm seriously irate —"

"I don't understand what I can do. If you get back to me later, then —"

"No, I'm in a hurry. I want to clear this up right now. If we can't, not a single person in that sauna will walk out of here alive. I have a rifle and a bazooka. I can blast that entire cottage to smithereens. If you don't believe me, keep an eye on the post next to you."

Nurmio steadied the rifle, aimed, and pressed the trigger. Through my binoculars, I saw splinters fly from the white wooden pillar. Nurmio's marksmanship left no room for complaint.

"Do you believe me now?"

"Yes. What do you want?"

"First of all, I want to know why someone wanted me dead. Secondly, I want to know why Jacobson and Oxbaum were killed. I was just supposed to scare them into keeping their mouths shut. Why wasn't that enough?"

Pensive silence.

"Speed it up. My trigger finger's getting itchy," Nurmio said.

"And I'm supposed to know?"

"The only ones who do know are you and Jakov. Jakov is way off in Israel, and you're here and in my sights. So you get to tell."

"You wouldn't dare shoot —"

Nurmio pressed the trigger and this time the bullet struck somewhere I didn't see. Levi evidently did, though, because he was examining the towel between his legs.

"You're insane! That almost hit me!"

194

"The next one is going to be aimed three inches higher. Your family jewels will become fish food."

"I had to… Jacobson would have talked anyway. I found out that he and Oxbaum had agreed that they would tell the police everything. Scare tactics wouldn't have worked. The mess had to be cleaned up, and for good. You know that Jakov and I have a lot of enemies in Israel. One tiny slip and they'll be after me —"

"And now everyone's after me instead. I was framed for two murders. That was a nasty trick."

"If you get out of Finland, I can guarantee you that —"

"If I were you, I wouldn't be making any promises. Why does Jakov want to get rid of me?"

"I don't know, believe me. I don't know."

"You'd better know. I'm in a nasty bind, but so are you. I was forced to kill that Belarussian hoodlum that Jakov sent after me. His body is in my office. Things like that are hard to explain to the Finnish police. I know what hard-asses they can be. Believe it or not, they won't even take money, no matter how much you try to push it on them." Nurmio looked my way and smiled.

"I can get you out of the country on an El Al flight," I heard Levi say. "I can make it happen tomorrow. I'll talk to Jakov and clear things up with him. This must be a misunderstanding. He'll listen to me. I promise —"

"You're a little too eager to make promises. Promises have a way of being forgotten in proportion to the number of feet from where they were made."

"The only thing I can think of is that Jakov doesn't trust you any more for some reason. You know that… know him…"

"I thought I did; I must not, after all. But evidently Jakov doesn't know me either, even though he should. I've done him some big favours and he betrayed me. He's going to pay for this, and so are you. You probably heard what I had to do for my citizenship. One crook and one politician won't weigh much in that equation. There's not a place on this earth Jakov could hide from me."

"Don't get worked up. We need to negotiate calmly."

"There's no time. The local police are on my ass. I want you to call Jakov as soon as you're done in the sauna and ask him about this, then you'll call me back right away. Tell him I want a good explanation, otherwise unpleasant things are going to happen, very unpleasant. I wouldn't want to cause a diplomatic incident between Finland and Israel, but if nothing else works, you'd better believe I will. We Finns don't make promises we can't keep."

"I'll try to call him. But you have to understand, he might not answer. He's so careful these days because —"

"I'm sure he'll take your call." Nurmio hung up.

I saw Levi glance in our direction. Then he disappeared into the sauna.

"Seemed to work like a charm," Nurmio said, looking satisfied with himself. "If we got all that on tape, that should already get us pretty far."

"We did," Sillanpää assured him.

"What do we do now?" I saw two security guards step out onto the porch. They were scanning the terrain with binoculars. Nurmio and Sillanpää also noticed them.

"We'd better get out of here," Sillanpää said.

"Why didn't you call Jakov directly?" I asked Nurmio once we were sitting in the car.

"There's always an intermediary. He doesn't answer calls himself – at least, not mine. If anyone can get through to him, it's Levi. I'm curious to hear the recording of that conversation. The tape will be the final nail in Jakov and Levi's coffins."

"Do you really believe that something like that will work in Israel?" Sillanpää asked doubtfully.

"I wouldn't be here without high-level support."

"The prime minister?"

"Something like that. Unfortunately I can't say any more about that."

"Then tell us about yourself. You left Finland a criminal and you came back practically a police officer. How did that happen?"

"My reputation as a criminal was hugely exaggerated," Nurmio said. "And there aren't any big secrets involved in my Israeli citizenship. This is for your ears only. During my stint in the UN, I did some big favours for them. When I headed to Israel, I looked up my old acquaintances. One of them had become a big boss in the Mossad. He thought I was a useful man, and hired me to work for his company. It's easier for a blue-eyed guy like me to travel around Arab countries where they don't look kindly on Jews. I did what I was supposed to do and was granted citizenship."

"If you manage to hook Jakov, how do you think you'll survive in Israel? If he's as powerful as they say, you're a marked man," Sillanpää said.

"I'm coming up to retirement age. Maybe I'll quit this business and come back to Finland. It's safe up here behind God's back. Or then I'll go somewhere else. I own a house in a place where oranges grow."

Nurmio's phone rang. "It's Levi."

Sillanpää pulled over at the side of the road.

"Did you get hold of Jakov?"

"Yes. He says he didn't send anyone after you. The sole targets were Jacobson and Oxbaum. It must have been a misunderstanding, or else there's something personal. Maybe you've stepped on someone's toes. He's sorry for the trouble he's caused you, and promised to compensate you generously. We agreed that I'd get you on an El Al flight to Israel. The Finnish authorities will have no way of getting at you there."

"That's very thoughtful of you, but my photo is in every paper and on television, and they know my name. How do you propose I'll get to the airport?"

"I made arrangements with the embassy to handle it. You'll get a new passport and diplomatic status. You can even spend the night there. You'll leave on the morning flight tomorrow. Rest assured: we brought Adolf Eichmann to Israel from Argentina, we'll get you from Helsinki to Tel Aviv. Are we set?"

"It doesn't feel like it. I don't trust Jacobson's son. Kazan is married to his sister."

"Don't worry about him. He's in this up to his neck, even though he doesn't know it."

"But he never paid back his loan to you."

"That gave us a good excuse to tell Oxbaum we no longer required his services. I don't have any more time to discuss this. Go straight to the embassy, and they'll take care of the rest."

"I guess I don't really have any choice. Thanks for the help."

"Remember, straight to the embassy. Do you understand?"

Nurmio hung up and smiled broadly. "The crooks are hooked."

Sillanpää started up the car and sped off.

"That's fantastic," I said. "Now for something a bit more unpleasant: we're going to have to arrest you on suspicion of the murder of Igor Semeyev."

I attended synagogue so infrequently that I felt guilty even when I did go, which made each subsequent visit more and more tortuous. Even this time, I wasn't at synagogue because of Rosh Hashanah; I was there for work. Haim Levi wanted to spend the holiday, which fell during his visit to Finland, at the Helsinki synagogue. Or I don't know if he wanted to, but he submitted to realities. Aside from being considered offensive, not attending synagogue would have demonstrated that Levi didn't honour his Jewishness. How could a man like that act as Minister of Justice, the judge of judges?

Rosh Hashanah, which fell in early September that year, marks the beginning of the ten days of repentance that come to their conclusion in Yom Kippur. During these days, after having weighed all of a man's deeds and thoughts, God decides whether his name will be recorded in the Book of Life or the Book of Death. Wrongdoers have reason to fear, ask for forgiveness and make restitution for their deeds. Debtors must pay their debts, quarrellers settle their quarrels.

Haim Levi had done so much wrong, and brazenly broken not only earthly but also divine laws, that I didn't believe ten days of repentance would suffice – even if he asked for forgiveness from dawn to dusk and dusk to dawn and recited a thousand *Kol Nidres*.

There was a large crowd in front of the synagogue, and more people kept arriving. The visit of the Minister of Justice of the Promised Land was an event that drew congregants who normally wouldn't have attended. Television fame has a strange effect on people. I was still a patrolman when the Palestinian leader Yasser Arafat visited Finland in 1989. Even though the Finns considered him a terrorist, throngs gathered to gawk everywhere he went. I was ordered to go to the Kalastajatorppa Hotel to meet his vehicle. Someone in police command evidently thought it would be a good joke.

A few months later, the Pope visited Helsinki, and once again folks were swarming all over the place, holding out their hands to shake his, even though only a handful of Finns are Catholics.

If the worst serial killer in history had been brought to the Jumbo shopping mall, the place would have been overrun with mobs of autograph-seekers. People hadn't changed a bit from the days when everyone went to the circus to be horrified by freaks disfigured since birth.

I was standing in front of the synagogue with Simolin, a few uniformed officers and a press photographer. The wind was blowing coolly from the north, and it felt as if the flu that had tried to grasp at me a few times was finally getting a proper grip. I was shivering and my throat felt gravelly.

A motorcade of motorcycle police and four black cars came from Fredrikinkatu and pulled up in front of the synagogue. Sillanpää and some other SUPO agent got out of the first car. Both wore the sunglasses that were the trademark of their profession. I could see Silberstein hurry across the yard to receive the arrivals. Josef Meyer and Eli followed at his heels, Eli looking somehow reluctant.

Two Israeli secret service men stepped out of the third car. They reacted to the environment clearly more suspiciously than Sillanpää and his companion. They came from a country where bombs and assassination attempts were not something you just read about in the papers; they were part of everyday life. That left a mark. That's why two security officers from the embassy had been to the synagogue that morning to go over the place with the SUPO security detail and a bomb dog. They had even checked and sealed the manholes in front of the synagogue.

The neighbouring buildings had been inspected carefully, all the way up to their attics, as had the guest list at the SAS Radisson hotel, where some of the rooms had line-of-sight views of the synagogue. These guys were real professionals.

The Israeli ambassador and Minister of Justice Haim Levi stepped out of the second car. The fourth car contained one more Israeli secret service man and the ambassador's family: his wife and two children. Levi waved at the curious congregants like he was Barack Obama visiting his hometown.

The party moved into the courtyard, where Silberstein was waiting. It must have been the first time I ever saw him so obsequious. Levi knew the protocol and shook hands with Silberstein first, then with Meyer, and finally extended his hand to Eli…

I looked at my brother, and it occurred to me that the last time I had seen that look on his face was when I had beaned him in the head with a snowball and then laughed. He had chased me around the yard, bellowing with rage and face contorted in fury. For a second I was sure that if he caught me, he would kill me. I was faster, and he didn't catch me, but I hadn't dared to approach him for hours afterwards.

I saw Levi stand there expectantly, hand extended. But Eli pulled his own hand back. It clenched into a fist, picked up speed and slammed into the corner of Levi's eye.

For a split second, the entire courtyard froze, colours faded, sound waves paused mid-air, and second-hands stopped ticking. Everything was suspended like that instant after a nuclear explosion before the blast of light strikes and the mushroom cloud rises from the ground. Then the moment passed and the secret service agents leapt into action. They dived for Eli and grabbed his hands. I rushed in and yelled: "I have him! It's OK! Look out for the minister!"

Eli writhed and looked at me with unseeing eyes. "Max was killed because of that shitbag… Let me go…" I clenched Eli tightly by the arm and led him off to the side. I managed to see a smile cross Sillanpää's face before civil servant officiousness washed it away. He came over and grabbed Eli by the other arm.

"What is this, some new kind of boxing diplomacy?"

Silberstein, pale as death and on the verge of fainting, looked on as the secret service agents wiped the blood from Levi's brow.

A second later, Levi started recovering from the shock of the blow. He pressed his forehead, looked around imploringly and kept begging: "Please, nothing happened here. I fell and hit my head. This stays between us… as long as you get that madman out of here. Having this get out won't be to anyone's advantage…"

Simolin and I led Eli to my car.

It had been a long time since I had been so proud of my brother.

EPILOGUE

It took over two months before the fuse that had been lit in Finland detonated a bomb in Israel.

The *Jerusalem Post* was the first to report that Haim Levi was suspected of criminal activity. The Minister of Justice had been escorted from his house for questioning over the acceptance of over two million dollars in bribes. Money had been distributed to several other power players in his party, too. The paper also reported that three well-known businessmen had been arrested on suspicion of bribery. Only two of the names were reported: Amos Jakov and Benjamin Hararin. But I knew the third one. It was Jacobson's son-in-law, Joel Kazan.

Nurmio had kept me up to date, which is why I was better informed than the *Jerusalem Post*, to whom the investigation had been leaked. The publicity ensured that the matter wouldn't be swept under the rug for the sake of political expediency. It took two more months before Levi resigned, even though the investigation was just beginning.

Here in Finland, things progressed much more rapidly. The investigation confirmed that Semeyev had killed Jacobson and Oxbaum. He had entered the Jacobson home from the back, using the spare key that was hidden outside. We suspected that Semeyev was told the location of the key by the homeowner's son-in-law, Joel Kazan. Threatening him with a gun, Semeyev had led Jacobson to the front door and shot him so it would appear as if Jacobson had opened the door for his killer. Semeyev had then returned to the back door and made his escape.

Soon afterwards, Nurmio had appeared and the neighbour keeping watch at the window had seen him. There was no way the timing could have been a coincidence. Someone wanted to make Nurmio a scapegoat, just as he had claimed.

The investigation of Semeyev's death had demanded high-level negotiations that also involved the participation of an official from the Israeli embassy. This part of the investigation was sealed for fifty years. In the closed-door trial, Nurmio was represented by my brother Eli.

A little before Christmas, I received a postcard from Nurmio. It had a picture of an orange tree laden with fruit. The stamp indicated that it had been sent from Portugal.

There was a brief note on the back: *Enjoying the sunshine. But then again, you never know... Shalom!*